FAMILY BLESSINGS

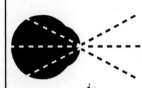

This Large Print Book carries the Seal of Approval of N.A.V.H.

FAMILY BLESSINGS

FERN MICHAELS

THORNDIKE PRESS

A part of Gale, Cengage Learning

GALE
CENGAGE Learning™

Detroit • New York • San Francisco • New Haven, Conn • Waterville, Maine • London

Copyright © 2004 by MRK Productions, Inc.
Thorndike Press, a part of Gale, Cengage Learning.

Thorndike Press® Large Print Famous Authors.
The text of this Large Print edition is unabridged.
Other aspects of the book may vary from the original edition.
Set in 16 pt. Plantin.

LIBRARY OF CONGRESS CATALOGING-IN-PUBLICATION DATA

Michaels, Fern.
  Family blessings / by Fern Michaels. — Large print ed.
    p. cm. — (Thorndike Press Large Print Famous Authors)
  ISBN-13: 978-1-4104-4282-6 (hardcover)
  ISBN-10: 1-4104-4282-9 (hardcover)
  1. Grandmothers—Fiction. 2. Pennsylvania—Fiction. 3. Christmas stories. 4. Domestic fiction. 5. Large type books. I. Title.
  PS3563.I27F36 2011
  813'.54—dc23   2011032084

Published in 2011 by arrangement with Pocket Books, a division of Simon & Schuster, Inc.

Printed in the United States of America
1 2 3 4 5 6 7 15 14 13 12 11

I would like to dedicate this book
to the real Father Stanley Drupieski

PROLOGUE

The First Commercial Bank of Larkspur, Pennsylvania, was small enough that when Dr. Joel Wineberg swooped through the doors in full Batman regalia, neither the bank personnel nor the bank customers paid much attention. They did wave and smile however. Everyone within a seventy-five-mile radius knew Dr. Wineberg dressed up for his pediatric patients, as did his nurse, who was known to be Tinkerbell on Mondays, Barbie on Tuesdays, and the Little Mermaid on Thursdays. On Wednesdays and Fridays she pretended to be Eloise or Cinderella, to every little girl's delight.

Joel moved quickly across the small lobby to the loan officer's room, where his best friend and colleague, Dr. Zack Kelly, was waiting for him. Norman Kellogg, the bank's only loan officer, stood as Joel entered. They shook hands all around, made small talk about the blustery weather conditions, and got down to business.

Norman Kellogg was a round man with a round bald head, a round cherubic face fitted with round wire-rim glasses. He was a happy man and would retire the first of the year. He was smiling as he held out pens to both Zack and Joel. "Just sign on the dotted line, boys, and you will be the proud owners of your first boat. I hope you invite me aboard one day."

Joel shoved his Batman cowl farther back on his head. He glared at his buddy, and hissed, "Tell me again why we're doing this."

Zack raised his hands in frustration. "You know why, Joel. Don't go getting cold feet now. It's my dream. You said it was your dream, too! We can do this. We're taking a year off and going sailing. All the details have been taken care of. We pick up our new boat January 3 in Miami, then it's the open sea for us! It's the wonder in wonderful! It's like a hundred Christmas mornings all rolled into one. We've taken classes all summer and fall. When we set foot on that boat, we'll be experts. Just sign your name, Joel."

Joel's eyes were wild as he stared at the colorful paintings of the Allegheny Mountains that adorned Norman Kellogg's office. "We took care of all the details but one," he grumbled again.

Zack tugged at his colorful tie. "If you're talking about our wives, get over it. They are going to be so happy when we surprise them, you'll see you worried for nothing."

"Oh, yeah, if they're going to be so happy, how come we didn't tell them at the outset? You need to think about how we're going to explain all those nights going to classes when we led our wives to believe we were working. Sara is on my case, and I know she's thinking terrible things. Once or twice she asked me if I was having an affair."

Zack shrugged, but his own eyes looked worried. "I have it all figured out. I convinced Jonesy to cover for me next weekend. I'm going to wine and dine Hannah and . . . and . . . spring it on her when she's in the right mood." He plucked a line from a commercial he'd seen, and said, "I know she'll embrace the whole idea because she knows it's my dream. Sign the damn paper, Joel."

Joel shuffled his feet, pursed his mouth, and looked over at his buddy. "You sign it first. This was all your idea. Yeah, yeah, I went along with it because you made it sound so damn good, and I am badly in need of some R&R. We should have told our wives. I just know we're going to regret this. Go ahead and sign, Zack."

Zack yanked at his tie again before picking up the pen. He was stunned to see that his hand was trembling. He was a surgeon, for God's sake. He was supposed to have nerves of steel. His hands never shook. Never. But they were shaking now. He took one long moment to think about star-filled nights aboard the boat making love to Hannah on deck. He scrawled his name, his eyes wilder than Joel's.

Done.

Joel signed his name. Norman Kellogg snatched the loan paper and pretended to blow on the signatures.

"You boys and First Commercial Bank of Larkspur are now co-owners of a new forty-foot cabin cruiser. I guess I should say Bon Voyage." He reached under his desk and brought up two boxes and two calendars for the new year. "It's a gift the bank gives out to loans over two hundred thousand dollars." Both doctors blanched at the amount of money they were borrowing. "Coffeemakers," Kellogg said proudly. Neither doctor made a move to accept the colorful boxes. "For the boat," Kellogg said.

"I knew that," Zack said.

"Yeah, I knew that, too," Joel said.

"Just give me another five minutes, and I'll have your copies ready for you. There's a warranty on those coffeepots, so be sure to send in the warranty cards," Kellogg said as he made his way over to the copy machine. "What are you going to call your new boat? It has to be a woman's name, you know."

Zack looked at Joel, and Joel looked at Zack.

"I see a problem here," Joel said. "If we name it the Hannah Sara, Sara will get ticked off because her name isn't first. If we name it the Sara Hannah, Hannah will get ticked off because her name isn't first. I hate you, Zack."

"Listen, Batman, you were just as eager to buy this boat as I was. A whole year away from here, away from kids, family, pressure. You loved the idea of sailing and sleeping under the stars and eating from the galley. Not to mention, sailing into little coves and exploring. Don't go sour on me now."

"We lied, Zack. We connived. We borrowed money and didn't tell our wives. This is going to hit them smack in the face. I hate you, Zack."

"It's only a year. The second year Jonesy and your guy are going to lease the boat. That means no payments the second year. The third year we're going to charter it out and make money. We get to sail it year four, then we trade it in for a *bigger* boat. The sea will be calling our names by then. The girls will be begging us to take another year off. It's a win-win situation."

"I still hate you. I have to get back to the office." Joel gave his Batman cape a wild swoosh as he snatched his copy of the loan agreement from Norman Kellogg's hands.

"Hold it, Batman!" Zack ran after him to hand over the coffeemaker. He was laughing so hard, he almost choked as Joel hid it under his black satin cape and dashed out of the office.

Zack settled himself in his car, the loan papers in his hands. Joel was right. They should have told the girls about the boat from the start. But he'd felt so sure that Hannah and Sara would want whatever he and Joel wanted. An uneasy feeling settled in the pit of his stomach. What would he do if Hannah balked? What if she didn't want to go away for a year? Ditto for Sara. He closed his eyes and shuddered. Would he go off without Hannah? Or would he have to charter out the boat or sell it?

Did I just make the biggest mistake of my life?

CHAPTER ONE

One Month Later

"It's hard to believe Halloween has come and gone already." Loretta Cisco, founder and recently retired CEO of Cisco Candies who was known as Cisco to her family, opened the screen door to let the dogs out. Freddie, a golden retriever, barked to let his partner, Hugo, know it was time to get a move on. It was the same thing as saying the breakfast bacon will still be there when we get back. Hugo, a black Lab, bolted through the door.

Ezra Danford, a tall, robust man, and Cisco's live-in companion, as well as partner, turned from the stove where he was making blueberry pancakes, Cisco's favorite breakfast. "I know what you mean, Loretta." He insisted on calling her by her given name, saying the pet name Cisco was just for her son and her grandchildren, the triplets, to use. "In a few weeks we'll be out there raking the last of the leaves and bringing in firewood. Then before you know it, the holidays will be here."

Cisco tugged at the apron she was wearing. "Time moves too fast when you're old, and we're old, Ezra. I dearly love the holidays, as you well know, but in another way they're sad because it means another year is coming to a close. You and I, my dear, also have an anniversary coming up. If the Trips," she said, referring to her triplet grandchildren, "hadn't brought you here that special Christmas almost three years ago, I might never have gotten to know you. For that, I will be eternally grateful."

Ezra expertly flipped a pancake, then turned the strips of bacon to the other side. "We should get married, Loretta." He winked at her, hoping she would get flustered and say yes.

Cisco adjusted the glasses perched on the end of her nose before she gave her colorful apron another hitch. "No, Ezra, we shouldn't get married. You had a wife, and I had a husband. When we depart this world, you're going with your wife, and I'm going with my husband. That's the way it has to be. Otherwise, your children and grandchildren will have a problem, as will mine. They won't know where to put us.

"We've talked about this a hundred times, Ezra. Why are you bringing it up again today? The relationship we have right now is working just fine for both of us. You know what happens when you tamper with something that doesn't need tampering with."

Cisco took her place at the table, the dogs' plates in her hands. Her gaze was drawn to the kitchen window. "Is it my imagination, Ezra, or does it look yellow outside?"

A puzzled look on his face, the man, who was as big as a bear, walked to the old screen door and opened it. It did look yellow outside. His eyes narrowed slightly. "Loretta, turn on the television or radio and let's hear the weather report. There might be a fire somewhere. I don't hear the birds either. It's much too quiet," he said, peering into the distance. "I know it's autumn, but it's strange. The winter birds love to nest in your old sycamore and sing to us every morning when we have breakfast. Some bad weather might be on the way." He called both dogs to come indoors.

"Are they saying anything on the TV?" Ezra walked out onto the back porch and looked around. The air was yellow as far as he could see. He stepped back in and looked at Cisco questioningly as the dogs whined at her feet.

Cisco poured syrup on her pancakes. "They haven't said a thing. We'll keep it on while we eat in case a bulletin comes in. We can't have bad weather today. The family is coming, and we're picnicking under the sycamore. A nice, long, lazy Sunday to enjoy having everyone here with us. It will probably be our last outdoor get-together before the cold weather sets in. There simply cannot be any bad weather today. I won't allow it," she said lightly.

Ezra ate quickly, something he never did. He loved food and always took his time when eating, enjoying every mouthful. When he finished, he picked up the dogs' plates and his own and stacked them in the dishwasher before he walked back to the door to stare at the yellow world outside the house.

He moved then, quicker than lightning. "Hurry, Loretta. I want you and the dogs to go down to the root cellar. I can't be certain about this, but the only time in my life that I saw a world of yellow was when I lived in Arkansas, and a tornado whipped through. Hurry now."

Cisco needed no second urging. She dumped her dishes in the dishwasher and herded the dogs down the cellar steps. "What are you going to do, Ezra?"

16

"Lock up, crack some of the windows. I'll be down in a minute. Take care of the dogs. Go to the southwest corner of the root cellar. Maybe I'm wrong, Loretta. It's better to be safe than sorry."

Cisco was at the bottom of the steps when she heard the sound. She knew instantly what it was. "Never mind the doors, Ezra, get down here. Now!"

Ezra was at the bottom of the steps the minute she finished speaking. The dogs whined and whimpered as Cisco led them down three more steps to the root cellar, where she kept her winter vegetables. The door was stout, with iron bars crisscrossing it from top to bottom.

The sound overhead increased in volume until it sounded like a hundred jet airplanes breaking the sound barrier. Ezra and Cisco clung together, their old bodies trembling as they tried to comfort one another and the dogs at the same time.

And then it was deathly quiet. The dogs yipped once, then were quiet.

Ezra struggled with the iron bars holding the door in place. When he finally got the door open, he was looking at the cellar staircase and nothing else. He could see the sky, the backyard, and the old sycamore. He tested the steps to make sure they were sturdy before he allowed Cisco and the dogs to climb them. He went first, ascending the steps carefully.

He looked around in stunned amazement. It was all gone, every last wall and window. What looked like half of the roof was on top of the barn, which itself was leaning drunkenly to the side. There was no sign of Cisco's car or his pickup truck.

Ezra's voice sounded choked. "This house was in the direct path, Loretta. It's all gone. Look up the hill; my house is still standing."

"It can't be gone, Ezra, it just can't," Cisco insisted as she looked around. She started to cry. Freddie hugged her leg, not understanding what was going on. Hugo pawed Ezra's leg for the big man to comfort him. "My whole life was here in this little house, Ezra. All the Trips' belongings were here as well as my son's from the day they were born. How can I ever replace them? Oh, Ezra, this is the worst thing that's ever happened to me. It's worse than when my son stuck me in that assisted-living facility. At least I could close my eyes and picture this beloved little house of mine. How can it all be gone, Ezra? *How?*"

All Ezra could do was put his arm around her shoulder, and murmur, "I don't know,

Loretta. I just don't know. Careful, watch your step now. Let's take a walk around. Maybe we can salvage something."

"I'm too old to start over, Ezra. Do you see my kitchen table anywhere? I started Cisco Candies in my kitchen on that old table. I kept the Trips' bassinet in the kitchen because it was the warmest room in the house during the winter. I diapered Jonathan there, too. Oh, God, how did this happen?" She looked around wildly as she staggered from one place to another, hoping to find something that belonged to her.

Ezra's voice was gentle, soothing, when he said, "You can rebuild the house and barn, Loretta. A good contractor can have it built for you by Christmas if the weather holds. I wouldn't be surprised if the whole town turns out to rebuild for you because you moved Cisco Candies here from New York City and provide employment for so many of the people in town. We can stay at my house while the building is going on. I know that's not what you want to hear, but it's the only consolation I can give you right now."

Cisco gave no indication she could hear what he was saying. Instead, her gaze raked the yard, hoping to see something from the house. She hated the way she was feeling,

19

hated the tears rolling down her wrinkled cheeks. Her voice was a whisper when she said, "Where do I go to get my memories back? I need to *touch* my things. I need to *see* them." She picked up the hem of her apron and wiped at her eyes. "Why, Ezra, why?"

Ezra wrapped his arms around her, his eyes full of sadness. "No one can take away your memories, Loretta. Your mementos, yes, but not the memories. It was an act of God, and we're both wise and old enough not to question Him. Now, pull up your socks, old girl, and let's walk around. I'm sure we'll find something." •

"One thing, Ezra. All I want is one thing. Something to hold in my hand. Please, help me. Please. I can't believe this. My whole life was in that house, and now it's gone. It's like it was never here. Like *I* was never here. It was here one minute, then in another minute it was gone." •

Ezra linked his arm with hers. He squeezed her hand to give her comfort. Together, they started off, their steps wobbly and unsure, the dogs trotting along beside them.

"We're in the valley, Ezra, why did it hit here and not the top of the hill where your house is? Why are the gardens and trees intact? I don't understand any of this. Look at the pumpkins! Even the leaves haven't been damaged. The holly trees are just as beautiful; so is the sycamore. Just my little house. Dammit, Ezra, this isn't fair!"

There was no answer, and Ezra didn't try to find one. All he could do was help Loretta search for her belongings.

"Freddie can't sleep without her blanket," Cisco said brokenly as she picked her way through debris. "I need my pillow. You need your slippers. You just got them broken in so they don't hurt your bunions."

"We'll buy new ones, Loretta. One can get used to anything. We're all alive. That's all that matters. Tomorrow we'll call a contractor I know and a salvage company. We're going to rebuild your house just the way it was. Maybe even better. Life will go on, Loretta, because that is the order of things. Now, I'm going to ask you one more time, and I'm never going to ask you again, so keep that in mind when you give me your answer. Will you marry me?"

Cisco stared up at the big man whom she loved so dearly. She was aware, for the first time, how vulnerable she was. She would never, ever, take anything for granted again. If it hadn't been for Ezra and his keen eye, they'd all be dead. "Yes, I will marry you on

21

Christmas Day," she responded smartly.

"Attagirl! Whoa, what have we here?" Ezra said as he heard the dogs barking furiously. "Follow the sound, Loretta. I don't know this for certain, but I think the dogs found something."

They ran as fast as their seventy-year-old bodies would permit. Cisco's disappointment was so keen, Ezra felt it. "It's my yellow teakettle. Look, the whistle is still on it. It wasn't exactly what I had in mind to hold in my hand, but it will do. I think it's as old as I am. Good girl, Freddie," Cisco said, reaching for the battered teakettle. "Where's Hugo?"

As if on cue, the black Lab trampled through a hedge of mountain laurel, dragging a string of Christmas lights. He dropped them at Cisco's feet and barked happily.

Cisco gathered up the string of lights with her yellow teakettle and held them close against her chest as though they were a lifeline. "I wonder if the lights work. We have to go to your house right now, Ezra, and plug them in. If they work, I think I can handle the rest of . . . *of this.*"

"Let's walk a little more, Loretta. We might find something else." The expression on Cisco's face made Ezra do an about-face. "On second thought, let's walk up to my house and turn on the television. We might as well find out the bad news now. I'm sure there were other houses in the path of the tornado. I want to see if those lights work, too. Christmas Day is going to be extraspecial this year, eh?"

Cisco squeezed Ezra's hand. "Yes, and I'm going to wear my old wedding dress. Hannah made me a white shawl last year for Christmas, and I'll wear it, too. Do you have your old wedding suit?" She started to cry again when she realized her old wedding dress and the white shawl were gone, along with everything else.

"I do! It might be a tad snug, but I'm game if you are."

A tired smile worked its way around Cisco's lips. "My dress would have been too snug anyway. Hannah and Sara wore it and had it taken in when they each got married. Their mother wore it, too. That old wedding gown had a lot of mileage on it. Do you think that's the order of things, too, Ezra? You know, the way it's supposed to be?"

Ezra didn't know if it was or wasn't. He opted to take the high road, and said, "I suppose." Cisco seemed satisfied with his answer as they trudged up the winding road to Ezra's house. The dogs scampered ahead, barking joyfully, certain this was a new adventure.

Inside Ezra's sparkling kitchen, Cisco looked around. "I don't like this kitchen, Ezra. It's right off the assembly line. It's so . . . so . . . *modern.* There's no character here, no memories. It's just a house. Why is that, Ezra?"

"Because it's only four years old. It's new, Loretta, built to my specifications. New is new. You and I can build a few memories here until it's time to move into your *new* house. It might be a good thing for both of us. Nothing is forever, as we just found out. What are you doing, Loretta?"

"I'm scrubbing the teakettle so I can make us a cup of tea. We have to have tea, Ezra. To . . . to . . . seal . . . oh, I don't know. I just feel like making us tea. Did you plug in the lights?"

"Yes! Turn around!"

"Oohhh, Ezra, they work. They actually work! How beautiful they look. Just looking at them makes me feel better. They have to be at least fifty years old, maybe more. Wrap them in tissue and put them somewhere safe. The Trips will want to see them. They are going to be so devastated when they get here."

"They're young, Loretta. I'm not saying they'll take it in stride, but they'll adjust better than you and I. Let's face it, we're set in our ways," Ezra said as he turned on the small television on the kitchen counter.

Cisco looked at him, a sour expression on her face. "What you mean is *I'm* set in my ways. Tell me something. Why do you need all these fancy appliances? Sub-Zero this, Sub-Zero that. What's wrong with Sears Roebuck appliances?"

Ezra threw his hands in the air. "I don't know, Loretta. The contractor installed them. I wasn't even here when the house was being built. You'll get used to them in time, and if you don't want to cook, then I'll cook. Oh, listen, they're talking about the tornado."

Cisco turned on the gas and set the yellow teakettle on the burner. They both stared at the television, their faces filled with horror. The news wasn't good. Seven houses in the path of the tornado were leveled. Four people were dead. Three people were missing. Seventeen cars simply disappeared off the face of the earth. Volunteers were asked to report to the school gymnasium to help aid the homeless victims. The Red Cross would be setting up a command center at City Hall.

"We can't even go into town to help since our cars are gone," Cisco said sadly. "As soon as the Trips get here, we'll go and do what we can. We . . . I don't have anything to donate, but I certainly have enough money to help out. Hannah is so good at doing things like that. We can put her in charge. Sara, too. Sam can scout around for living accommodations for the homeless, and I'll pay the rents. Zack and Joel can offer medical services since both of them are doctors. Jonathan . . . well, Jonathan can work on the transportation end of things. We're part of this community, and we have to do everything we can.

"Did you think Hanny looked *twitchy* last week when she stopped by? And Sam was almost surly. I wonder if it's my imagination. I always knew what was going on with my grandchildren, but since they all got married I'm . . . what is it the young people say these days? Out of the loop."

Ezra scratched his head. Sometimes Loretta moved and did things at the speed of light, and he had to struggle to catch up. "As I recall, Hanny did seem a little jittery. Is it possible she's pregnant? Sam now, that's something else. I think he's struggling with something, and, whatever it is, he's holding it close to his chest. At least for now."

"No, Hanny is not pregnant. When you're pregnant, you're so beautiful you just glow. Your eyes sparkle with happiness. Hanny doesn't look like that. I don't know, Ezra, maybe she's having trouble adjusting to being married. After all, she's only been married ten months." Cisco couldn't help but smile as she remembered the triple wedding that took place last New Year's day. Hannah had wed Zack Kelly, the ophthalmologist who had removed Cisco's cataracts at Larkspur Community Hospital; Sara had wed Joel Wineberg, a pediatrician affiliated with the hospital; and Sam had married Sonia, the Ukranian exchange student he'd fallen for at Penn State. What a memorable day it had been. So much happiness. Now, she turned her gaze back on Ezra, and said, "As you know, my granddaughter Hannah is tart-tongued. The children called her Hard-Hearted Hannah from the time she was little. She takes no prisoners. Hanny is a 'what you see is what you get' kind of person. She wasn't like that during our visit. She was quiet and spent a lot of time staring out the window. I think she's worried about something. Sam . . . I just don't know." She shook her head in bewilderment.

Ezra was grateful Loretta was talking

about something other than the loss of her beloved little house in the valley. Having raised the triplets after their mother's death, she was more mother than grandmother to them and worried constantly even though they were twenty-five years old. Some things, he knew, would never change.

He wished his own children, who lived in California, were closer to him. He told himself they had their own lives just the way his grandchildren had their own lives. They called on Father's Day and Christmas, but that was it. He'd been stunned when Loretta and her little family had welcomed him with open arms. He could still remember her words as if it were yesterday. "I'd be more than happy to share my family with you, Ezra. We have more than enough love to go around. One more will fit very nicely into our lives. And, we adore your dog!" He'd actually blushed, then felt like beating his chest in some primal way to show how much he'd come to love them all.

He needed to say something reassuring to Loretta now before she got carried away. She was right, though, Hanny hadn't been herself the last time she visited. "I think Hannah is like most young people, Loretta. She's busy and tries to fit everything into a twenty-four-hour period when she really

28

needs thirty-six hours." He didn't want to think about Sam because Sam worried him, and he didn't know why.

"I have an idea. The family isn't going to be here for a few hours. They may not even know what happened yet. What do you say to my getting out the old tractor mower and we take a spin into town? It'll be slow going, probably around three miles an hour or so. We should get there around noon if we leave now. You might want to pack a lunch." Ezra guffawed. If he was hoping for a laugh or a rich chuckle from Cisco, he was disappointed. She was a million miles away in her memories.

"All right, Ezra. We might even meet up with the Trips while we're there. Just let me get changed. What *does* one wear for a ride on a tractor into town?"

Ezra eyeballed her to see if she was trying to be humorous or not. He decided she wasn't. "I suppose whatever one can find. You do have clothes upstairs, Loretta."

"I know, Ezra, I know. I'm sorry I'm not acting . . ." Her voice trailed off to nothing.

"Loretta," Erza said patiently, "I know how you all loved that little house. As hard as it is for you to believe or understand, you have to make the effort to come to terms with the loss. Everything happens for a reason. Most times a person never finds out the reason until much later, then they go, 'ah, now I understand.' Tomorrow the sun is going to come up, and we'll decide what to do. Your family will be arriving soon, and you'll want to discuss matters with them. For now, we'll just muddle through."

Cisco reached up to touch Ezra's cheek. "What would I do without you, Ezra? I don't care about the sun coming up tomorrow. Well, I do, but I just want you to know that you are the sunshine of my life. After everyone leaves this evening, I'm going to bake you a wonderful blackberry pie, and you and I are going to eat the whole thing."

Ezra smiled. "I thought the family was staying overnight."

"Well, we'll just have to shoo them out. You don't have enough room in this house for everyone. I'm going to bake you that pie, and that's final."

"With ice cream and vanilla-flavored coffee?" Ezra asked hopefully.

"Absolutely," Cisco said. "I'll be ready in a few minutes. Get the mower out. We have to leave the dogs here of course."

Ezra knew she was just going through the motions and saying words she thought he wanted to hear. "I'll get the mower." If Cisco heard him, she gave no sign.

Two hours later Ezra steered the John Deere tractor mower down Main Street. No one paid them the least bit of attention.

Nestled in the foothills of the Allegheny Mountains, Larkspur was a pretty little town with a town square where all public functions were held. The Fourth of July picnic was always a rousing success, with banners and American flags everywhere and a hundred percent turnout of the citizenry. The parade down Main Street was full of homemade floats, the school band, the football team, and baton twirlers.

Hot dogs, hamburgers, corn on the cob, and root beer slushes were the food and drink of the day. At night, from seven till nine, there was a square dance in the pavilion for the older folks. From nine to eleven, the pavilion was turned over to the younger set and a local band named Fred Fish and the Merry Minnows, which the youngsters rocked and rolled to until they were dizzy. It was the highlight of the year.

Then again, the older folks said that Christmas was the highlight of the year, with the live Santa, who sat in his sleigh for twenty-one days, handing out candy canes until the moment that the carolers took over on Christmas Eve, when, once again, the whole town turned out, this time to join the carolers before going to midnight services at the churches that held them.

It was a sleepy, comfortable little town, where everyone knew everyone else. A town where people cared about their neighbors and offered to help the minute things went awry, which wasn't often.

Today, the town was a beehive of activity, with television trucks, satellite dishes, and news media there to cover the deadly tornado.

"The last time I saw this many people in town was the Fourth of July," Cisco said, as Ezra helped her down from the mower. "I think we should find the mayor and go from there. What do you think, Ezra? I don't see the children anywhere. We should have left a note on your door. Why didn't we do that, Ezra?"

"We just forgot, Loretta. Come along."

"I'm coming, Ezra, hold your horses," Cisco shot back with a smidgin of her old spirit.

The blue BMW wound its way down the road, then accelerated up the rise. When Sara Cisco Wineberg reached the crest, she sucked in her breath and let out a scream that could be heard from one end of the valley to the other. "Look, Hanny! Oh, my

Godddd!"

Hanny opened the door and started to run, Sara on her heels. "The house is gone!" she screamed shrilly. "Where are Cisco and Freddie? Sara, say something. Tell me they're all right. Please, tell me they're all right," she continued to scream shrilly.

Sara started to cry. "How can I tell you something like that?" She started calling out to her grandmother, but there was no response. "I heard about the tornado on the news, but I never thought . . . I just didn't think . . . oh, God, not Cisco. Someone should have called us. Come on, Hanny, we have to look for them. It's gone," she babbled. "It's all gone. Even the fireplace is gone." She called out again, this time more shrilly. Hanny joined in.

"Why didn't they call us to say they were okay?" Hanny bleated. She picked up a stick and whacked at a sapling. "I don't see any of our stuff. What happened to the washing machine? The refrigerator, our beds, the furniture? Did they just fly through the air? What? Dammit, I need to know, Sara."

Sara sat down on a tree stump and stared up at her sister. She was already hoarse from all the shouting. "I don't know the answer, Hanny. I don't know much of anything these days. My husband should be here; so should your husband. And where the hell is our brother Sam? It would be nice to see Dad, too. They must have heard the news like we heard it, so why aren't they here?"

Hannah sat down on the ground and hugged her knees. Like her sister, she was hoarse from shouting. "Let's go up to Ezra's house. Maybe they're up there. It's still standing, I can see the roof from here. They aren't dead, Sara. I'd feel something if they were, and so would you. But, to answer your other question, I don't know why my husband isn't here. He had to work today, even though it's Sunday. That's all he does, work. I hardly ever see him. Sam said he was leaving early to come out here. Maybe he's with Cisco and Ezra." She stood up and reached for Sara's hands to pull her to her feet.

Sara sprinted off, her mouth going a mile a minute. "Please let them be alive and well. Please, please, please."

"Where's Joel?" Hannah asked at the halfway mark up the hill.

"The same place your husband is, the hospital. I never see him, like you never see Zack. This marriage business isn't what it's cracked up to be. I cook dinner and eat it by myself. I go to bed by myself. When I wake up, Joel is gone. He leaves me notes. I thought it would get better, but it isn't. I'm seriously thinking about asking for a divorce. I can't live like this anymore. How do you do it, Hanny? Oh, God, is that Freddie barking? It is! They're here! They're here, Hanny!"

They both ran then, across the yard and up the long driveway, as though they had wings on their feet. They skidded to a stop when they saw a dark green Range Rover crawling up the hill behind them.

"Sam!" the girls said in unison.

"Yep, it's me. I've been down in the valley searching. I found this," he said, holding out a yellow ribbon with a bell on it."

"That was my first hair ribbon. Mom put a bell on it so she could find me," Sara said, bursting into tears. "She said I always wandered off."

"Freddie's here, so that has to mean Cisco and Ezra are here, too. They wouldn't have left the dogs alone. They're safe, I know it," Sara said, breathing hard. "Can't you hear Freddie barking?"

Sam climbed out of the truck. He was dressed in jeans and a white T-shirt. His curly hair was cropped short and smashed down with a Pittsburgh Pirates baseball cap. "That sound is music to my ears. When I pulled up to the rise earlier, I almost died when I didn't see the house. I think I went a little nuts there for a minute."

"So did we," Sara said. "Where's Sonia?"

"She's packing to go back home. That's another way of saying she's leaving me. Now, do you want to talk *that* to death, or do you want to find Cisco and Freddie?" Sam asked, his tone of voice frigid.

Hanny stopped in her tracks. It seemed to her in that one instant that her whole life was unraveling. The house was gone, Cisco and Freddie were missing, Sara was talking about getting a divorce, and now Sam was saying Sonia was leaving him. On top of that, she had her own miserable problem with Zack to deal with.

"Divorce is such a terrible . . . ending. I thought you were happy," she muttered.

"I was. Obviously, Sonia wasn't. Is the door locked?"

"Get real, Sam. No one in Larkspur locks their doors. Open it!"

The dogs leaped and pawed at them, barking joyously as Sara ran through the house searching for her grandmother. She was back in the kitchen within minutes. "They're not here, but Cisco's clothes are. Maybe they had enough time to get to the root cellar, and when it was over they came up here. Cisco must be devastated. Hell, I'm devastated. Dad's coming, isn't he?"

Sam was on the floor, Freddie in his lap. He stroked the silky dog, his eyes moist. "He said he was."

Hanny turned on the television to the local station. The trio sat and watched, their eyes wide with the devastation they were seeing. "Nothing like this has ever happened around here."

Sam's voice was so bitter-sounding, his sisters cringed. "There's a first time for everything, I guess."

Hanny thought about her brother's words. A first time for everything. It was so true. She bit down on her bottom lip. The urge to cry was so strong, she bit down harder and tasted her own blood. "You're right, Sam. There's a first time for everything."

She jumped up, jamming her hands into the pockets of her khaki slacks.

"You look like you lost some weight, Hanny," Sara said.

"Well, I didn't. It's your imagination. I eat like a horse," Hannah lied. She couldn't remember the last time she'd eaten a solid meal.

Sara blinked, her expression confused. "Hey, I just made a comment, okay? You don't have to bite my head off."

"Sorry, Sara. I'm just worried," Hannah said.

"Now that that's out of the way, let's pile into my Range Rover and go to town to see if Cisco is there with Ezra. I'm thinking they'd both go there first thing to see if they could help. C'mon, guys, let's go," he said to the anxious dogs. "It's time to find Cisco."

CHAPTER TWO

Sam Cisco steered his SUV to a slow crawl, tapping the horn ever so lightly to urge the throngs of people to step aside so he could park his vehicle. He wanted to concentrate on the tragedy and do what he could to help, but his thoughts were with his young wife, who was preparing to return to Europe. Or so she said.

From early childhood on, his sisters had told him, usually on a daily basis, that he was stupid, and they were smart. He knew then just the way he knew now, that they were just words. Was he stupid? Why didn't he see this coming? After he'd married Sonia he'd been happier than a pig in a mudhole. So where did it all go wrong? He wished he knew. Maybe Hanny and Sara could tell him. Then again, did he really want to hear the two of them bash him the way they always did even though it was good-natured? He hated telling Cisco because she loved Sonia like a daughter. Would she blame him the way he was blaming himself?

Sam was shaken out of his reverie when Hanny screeched in his ear. "There's a parking place. Move, Sam!"

Sara looked around in awe. "I think the whole town is here in the square." Everywhere as far as the eye could see, little knots of people with clipboards gestured and pointed. A small town coming together to help each other. All the stores were open, even though it was Sunday, and they were supposed to be closed. The doors of John Mitchell's hardware store were wide-open. He was handing out rakes, shovels, and wheelbarrows, barrels of nails and hammers, and anything else people needed. Sara knew there would be no charge. John Mitchell was like that.

At Finnegan's Emporium, workers were handing out work gloves, sweat bandannas, and anything people asked for. Again, there would be no charge, just as there would be no charge for the sandwiches and coffee from Mabel's Diner.

Freddie barked as she pawed the window in the cargo hold. Hanny turned around to see why the golden retriever was barking and saw Cisco and Ezra standing next to the parish priest, Father Drupieski, and Hiram Holloway, the town's mortician. "There's Cisco and Ezra! They're alive! Will you park this damn thing and let me out already!"

The Trips hit the ground running. They were children again, frightened out of their wits just the way they had been frightened out of their wits when they were little, and the only person who could make things right was Cisco. They hugged and kissed her, squeezing and pummeling her as they hung on to her arms for dear life. The dogs barked and whined to be included. Everyone obliged.

"The cavalry has arrived," Ezra said happily.

When Cisco could catch her breath, she said, "Freddie found my yellow teakettle, and Hugo found a string of Christmas lights. And they work. So, we didn't lose *everything*." She looked around, noticing for the first time that the Trips were partner-free. "Where are your spouses?"

The Trips eyed one another and suddenly started asking questions about what they could do to help. Cisco frowned, and with a nudge from Ezra refrained from asking any further questions.

"Ezra will tell you what to do. I'm going

41

with Hiram over to the mortuary to help . . . to do whatever I can for the families . . . of . . . of those who . . . who didn't make it. Father Stanley knows what has to be done." She smiled up at the priest, who was as old as she was. He'd married her son Jonathan and Margie, and christened the Trips. At least once a month he came for dinner and always brought a posy with him. Only Ezra knew that in private she called her old friend Drupi. "Do everything he says." She squared her shoulders imperceptibly, and said, "This is our little town. Our roots are here. Our friends need us right now."

The Trips watched Cisco move off. This was so like their grandmother. Her beloved home, their home, too, for many, many years, was gone, and she was only thinking about helping others.

Everyone knew the town of Larkspur would have withered and died if Cisco hadn't moved her candy factory and the company's corporate offices here over her son's objections. And she'd never asked the town government or the townspeople for a thing in return, just a day's work for a day's pay. Even when there were no job openings, if someone in town needed a job, Cisco created one for the applicant. She also provided health care, pension plans, and wonderful working conditions, as well as free Cisco Candies for the townsfolk.

Ezra looked down at the clipboard he was holding in his hand with no idea how or where he came by it. The writing was his own, so he must have made a list at some point. He started to rattle off instructions. The Trips listened intently, then scattered to do Ezra's bidding. Freddie and Hugo stayed at his side.

Father Drupieski turned away, out of the sun. "I must be going, too, Ezra. I'm needed over at the church. Please tell Loretta I will formally thank her for her monetary help next Sunday. There's no way this little town could . . ."

Ezra placed one of his big hands on the priest's arm. "Whatever you need, it's yours. Loretta said everything was to go through your hands. It's not that she doesn't like the Red Cross, she does. She just thinks this is our little town, and we take care of our own."

The old priest nodded. There were a few in town who thought Ezra had hitched his star to Cisco's wagon because of her money. He knew better. Ezra was almost as wealthy as Loretta Cisco, having made his fortune ranching and drilling oil in Wyoming. He did almost as much for the town as Loretta did but always quietly and anonymously. He even doubted Loretta knew that Erza was paying for at least a dozen different young people's college educations. She probably didn't know he had bought Louis Merriman a new tractor, and he knew for a fact that she didn't know he'd paid for Bertha Appleton's heart surgery three months ago. Hells bells, even Bertha didn't know who'd paid for her surgery. Every Sunday he felt it was his duty to announce the mysterious benefactor's good deeds from the pulpit without announcing a name.

Father Stanley Drupieski gave himself a mental shrug as he said good-bye to Ezra and headed for his little white church, which was badly in need of a coat of paint. The paint didn't matter; what mattered was giving comfort to those who were waiting for him. With the robust checks from Loretta and Ezra, he could now make and fulfill promises to those in need.

Dr. Zack Kelly looked just as cranky and tired as his companion, slash, best friend, and brother-in-law, Dr. Joel Wineberg. "I don't know why we're even bothering to go out to the valley. It's late, everyone will have eaten and be packing up to go home. Tell me again why we're doing this?" He yanked at his tie and threw it in the backseat. "In addition, no one goes to a barbecue/picnic in a suit, shirt, and tie. We're going to look like misfits."

Long years of familiarity allowed Joel to vent. "Just shut up, Zack. We're going because we promised we'd go. Right now I am number one on Sara's shit list. I need to correct that, and this picnic is the start." He, too, yanked at his tie and tossed it over his shoulder. For some reason Zack looked pleased at his friend's words. He stared at him suspiciously.

"Oh, yeah. You didn't tell me there was trouble in Paradise. I bet you five bucks I can top whatever the hell you're going to tell me. Fire away, buddy."

Joel slumped down in his seat, his long legs extended. "I haven't seen, that's as in *seen,* Sara in about ten days. She's in bed when I get home, which is around midnight, and she's asleep when I get up at five. Sometimes I think she's pretending. Gone are the days when she waited up for me and got up to cook me breakfast. Every kid within a hundred-mile radius seems to be sick. The life of a pediatrician is not an easy one.

"I have an associate and can't see my way to taking on another one. I need more hours in the day. That boat business is killing me. I have to tell Sara, and I can't get up the nerve. Everything started to go wrong when we began those night classes.

"Sara cooks dinner. Well, she did. The problem was, I was never home to eat it. She'd save it, but it would be dried out by the time I got to it. Now she doesn't even cook. She used to leave me little notes with smiley faces. She doesn't do that anymore either. Twice she used the D word. Do you believe that?

"And it's all because of that damn boat, Zack. I wish now we'd never bought it."

Zack shuddered at the misery in his friend's voice. Every man alive knew what the D word meant. Divorce. So far Hanny hadn't said the D word out loud, but he'd seen it in her eyes. She was just as fed up with him as Sara was with Joel.

"Yeah, sure I believe it. We work ten hours a day, then take all those nautical classes into the night. Look at it from their perspective. They're alone all the time. If it's any consolation to you, Joel, my good friend, my own wife seems to have some issues, too. I'm sure she and Sara commiserate on a daily basis. I'm starting to think plumbing might have been a better business to go into than the medical profession."

Outrage registered on Joel's face. "Are you kidding? Plumbers get called out in the middle of the night. I can't see myself crawling under a house to check pipes. I only told you all that thinking you might have some advice."

Zack took his eyes off the road for a second. "Well, you thought wrong, pal. Hanny should have called me on the cell phone by now. The truth is, she never calls me anymore. We're old married men now. The bloom is off the rose. I read that in a magazine one time." He screwed up his face as though he were in pain.

Joel reached over to adjust the heating unit. "Is that supposed to make me feel better? You know what else," he said, lowering his voice to a self-conscious hiss, "I wanted sex three days ago. Sara jabbed her elbow so hard into my ribs I have a bruise the size of a grapefruit."

Zack clucked his tongue in sympathy, his own expression as miserable as his friend's. "I guess you told me that to see if I'd confide in you, right? Well, guess what, I haven't had sex in over a month. We're young, we're supposed to be screwing our brains out like rabbits do. Something went wrong here, Joel, and I don't think we can blame it all on the boat. I feel undercurrents here," he said dramatically. "Now, are you happy that I spilled my guts?"

"No."

Zack floundered. "Maybe we should talk to Sam. He knows the girls better than anyone. Maybe he can offer some suggestions. Look, I know you love Sara as much as I love Hannah. We have to get back on track here before it's too late."

Joel hooted his disgust at his best friend's suggestion. "And you really think old Sam is going to be on our side? You're thinking this is a guy thing, right? Like we're all going to share and make things peachy perfect. Just get that thought right out of your head, buddy. He's one of three. A triplet. They're linked by some invisible bond you and I have no clue about. We're on our own."

"Now that scares the hell out of me," Zack said as he pressed his foot on the gas, blasted the horn, and swerved around a tractor trailer so he could make the turnoff that would lead him to Cisco's house in the valley.

"Down the hill, and up the rise, and then we reach grandmother's house," he said, his voice chilly with anxiety. "I wonder who got hit with that tornado. I heard about it from one of the nurses as I was leaving the hospital, but she didn't know the details of what happened."

"Whoa," Joel said, staring out the windshield from the top of the rise. "It's gone, Zack! The house is gone!"

"Oh, my God!" Zack stopped the car and got out. "Ezra's house is still standing. Man, that tornado must have cut a pretty wide swath. I wouldn't think a house down that low would get hit. That has to mean every house on that back road got leveled. Cisco . . . You don't think . . . Nah, nothing happened to her. We would have heard. Ezra's house is still standing. We should check it out. We *are* doctors. If there's anything good about this, it's that the Trips weren't heading this way till around noon. That means they're all right." He turned to look at Joel's pale face. He snapped his fingers. "We would have heard something otherwise. Look alive here, buddy. I'm telling you, they're all right. I just know it."

"I loved that house, I really did. It was so homey, so comfortable, so lived in. You just knew when you opened the door, you were welcome. How could something so wonderful, so right, be gone like that?" Joel asked.

The two men looked at one another, their eyes miserable. Each was thinking how right and wonderful their marriages were in the beginning. How full of warmth and laughter they were.

"I feel like bawling for some reason," Zack said as he switched gears to drive to the top of the second hill, where Ezra's house stood. It only took them five minutes to realize no one was home.

"Come on, we're going to town," Zack said, getting into the car.

It was midnight when the clan gathered in Ezra's heated sunroom, which had a view of the entire valley. Cisco, her snow-white topknot wiggling precariously on top of her head, looked from one to the other of the triplets. "You are more than welcome to stay. We certainly have enough beds and food. Ezra is defrosting tomorrow's dinner as we speak. I think we all did a good job today. Would anyone like some blackberry brandy? Ezra made it himself." For the first time in her life, Cisco hoped her family would turn down her invitation to stay overnight. She couldn't ever remember feeling as tired or sad as she felt now. All she wanted to do was go to bed, pull up the covers, and sleep for a week.

"Joel and I have to leave, Cisco," Zack said. "We have to be at the hospital at six. We both appreciate the invitation, though. We can come back next weekend to help if you need us."

Sara looked across the patio to where her husband was standing. "Hanny and I are staying here. What about you, Sam?"

"I'll let you know in a minute. I have to call Sonia." He ran into the house and called his own house. Either Sonia was gone, or she was sleeping. He prayed she was sleeping and would pick up the phone. After the fifteenth ring, his face white, he trotted out to the patio. "I'm staying," he said curtly.

"I guess you guys better get going," Hanny said, in a voice so cold it could have chilled milk. She tugged at the bright red turban covering her head. "You certainly don't want to be late for morning rounds." She waved airily as she tugged at Sara's arm. "Come and help me put sheets on the beds."

Ezra pinched Cisco's arm lightly and whispered in her ear. "This might be a good time to make our little announcement."

Cisco nodded. "Before you leave, Ezra and I have something to tell you. I'm sorry your father isn't here to hear it too, but he refused to leave the cleanup brigade. Ezra asked me to marry him, and I said yes. The wedding will take place on Christmas Day."

She held out her arms expecting the Trips

51

to step into her waiting embrace. Instead all she heard were some low-voiced comments that sounded like congratulations. And then the girls left the room, and Sam said he was going back to town to help his father.

Cisco eyed the two disheveled young men in wrinkled suits standing by the railing. "Does either one of you want to say anything?" she asked briskly.

Zack ran his hand through his hair. "Ah . . . no, Cisco, not at this time. I'm real happy for you and Ezra. Christmas Day is a great day for a wedding. At least you'll never forget your anniversary date."

"I'm real sorry about your house, Cisco. I know what it means to you and the Trips. I'm sure the builders will be able to rebuild it just the way it was. I think I'll say good night now," Joel said.

Cisco and Ezra accepted hugs from the two young doctors before they followed them out to the driveway. Their good-byes were quiet and subdued. Ezra wrapped his arm around Cisco's shoulder as they watched the red taillights of the departing car until they were nothing more than pinpoints in the dark night. "Morning will be time enough to talk about this, Loretta. I'll run a bath for you. Would you like some hot chocolate or perhaps a cup of chamomile tea?"

Cisco nodded. "You make the tea, Ezra, and I'll run my own bath. I'm so glad you never sold this house. If you had, we'd be living in a tent right now." Her voice was beyond weary when she said, "Tell me again why you didn't sell it when you moved into the cottage with me."

"You told me to keep it in case you ever got mad at me so I'd have a place to go." He chuckled at the memory. Cisco just nodded as she made her way up the steps, Freddie and Hugo behind her.

Cisco's thoughts weren't on why Ezra had kept the house or her part in his decision to hold on to it. Nor were her thoughts on her beloved little house in the valley. Her thoughts were on the Trips and the trouble she saw in their eyes. But, as Ezra said, tomorrow was another day.

And tomorrow, she was shutting down the factory and requesting that all employees turn out to help with the cleanup. They had to get things back to normal as soon as possible. Did it really matter if some of the candy shipments were late? No, it did not matter. Family and friends always had to come first no matter what.

Cisco rubbed at her temples as the tub filled with hot water. She wished she had some bubble bath. When was the last time she'd taken a bubble bath? She couldn't remember. In the great scheme of things, it simply wasn't important.

As Cisco lowered her arthritic body into the steamy water, she thought about how quiet the house was. *Where are the girls? Curled up on one of the beds telling each other their secrets.* And she knew there were secrets.

The moment she saw Freddie's ears perk up she knew Sam was home. Maybe the volunteers in town had gone home for the night? She shrugged. Sam needed to be with his sisters. He was part of the secret, and trouble always came in threes.

Always.

Sara and Hanny were wide-eyed when Sam blasted through the door. Sam never entered a room, he blasted through. "They had the night shift covered. Dad sent me home. Jeez, when was the last time we had a sleep-over like this?"

Hanny tugged at the pajamas she was wearing, which were at least six sizes too big for her. Her voice was sad when she said, "The last time was when we wanted to spring Cisco from the assisted-living facility Dad stuck her in. We really pulled together that time.

"Why is Sonia leaving you, Sam?" Hannah asked bluntly.

Sam sat on the floor Indian fashion. "Why don't we just say I blew it and let it go at that."

Sara picked up one of the pillows with little purple flowers on it, and said, "Because I don't believe it. Didn't you see it coming? You aren't *that* dumb."

Sam hung his head. "Well, guess what, I am that dumb because, no, I did not see it coming. Sonia can't . . . she said she couldn't adjust . . . to life here in a small town. She wants more. Action! She wants life. Activity. At least that's what she told me. I told her to do some volunteer work. She misses her parents. She misses her friends from school. I did everything I could. I took her out to dinner three or four times a week. We went to the movies. We went away for weekends. I gave her a good life. She has her own car, I made no demands on her. She had charge cards, and she used them. She wanted a baby right away. I wanted to wait. To answer your question, no, I didn't see it coming.

"Now that you've picked my brain, what's with you two? I've seen misery, and then there's misery, but nothing like what I'm seeing in you two. You should be sitting on top of the world. Literally." His voice was so cool and flat his sisters just stared at him.

Sara crunched the pillow even tighter to her chest. "My husband is sitting on top of the world. I'm at the bottom. He is the most-sought-after pediatrician within a hundred-mile radius. He leaves the house at five in the morning and doesn't get home till midnight. You tell me what kind of life that is for a newly married couple. If I gave Joel an ultimatum, his practice or me, which I would never do, he'd pick his practice. I haven't had a life for the past year. Yes, I know I married a doctor, and yes, I expected late hours once in a while. But when Joel is home, he spends all his time on the phone checking up on his patients because they're important to him. I want to be important to him, too. I want to be able to talk about my day, my family, us. He doesn't want to hear it. I don't like unsatisfying sex at four o'clock in the morning. On top of that, I think he's harboring some kind of secret. There, that's my story."

Sam and Hanny digested this confession, their eyes glued to their sister. Their heads bobbed up and down to show they understood and that, right or wrong, they were on her side.

Knowing it was now her turn, Hanny burst into tears. "My story is the same as Sara's. Zack is never home. There are so many demands on his time because he's such a fine surgeon. He has office hours all the time. I never see him either. But there's . . . there's something else."

"Oh, my God, you're pregnant!" Sara squealed.

"I should be so lucky. I think Zack is having an *affair,* and I think Joel is, too!"

Sara blinked.

Sam's eyes were so round they looked like balls of blue fire. "Where . . . how . . . You're nuts! Those guys don't have time to have affairs," he blustered in his brothers-in-law's defense.

Sara pushed the pillow into Hanny's face, and hissed, "You're lying! Tell us right now, this second, that you're lying, or Sam won't have to kill you, I'll do it myself. This is not funny, Hanny."

Hanny cried harder.

They were on her then, like white on rice, kissing her and hugging her, saying comforting words none of them would remember later.

"What makes you think such a thing?" Sara finally managed to gasp.

"Tell us," Sam said.

"Because I hear him whispering on the phone with Joel. Some woman called the house, and when I asked who she was, she refused to identify herself. I'm not stupid. I called the hospital many nights when Zack said he was working. Well, guess what, he wasn't working, and neither was Joel because I asked. Then I called you, Sara, and you said Joel was on call at the hospital. I tried following Zack one night, but once we hit the interstate, I lost him. He didn't come home that night until after midnight. On top of that, Zack bought new underwear. Colored. Calvin Klein. I always bought his underwear, and he liked white Fruit of the Loom. Now, what do you have to say?"

Sara swiped at the tears rolling down her cheeks. "They say the wife is always the last to know. I can't believe Joel would do this to me. Are you sure, Hanny? I mean are you *really* sure?"

"What other explanation can there be? Zack has been so . . . so secretive these past four months. Every time I ask him what's wrong, he withdraws or picks a fight. That's a clue right there. The underwear is the clincher, though. I read in *Cosmo* about how men start paying attention to their underwear when they have extramarital affairs."

Sam stared at his sisters, bug-eyed, as he wondered about his wife's fidelity. He voiced the thought. His sisters glared at him. "Of course it's the same for women. They buy lacy underwear and get new perfume. That was in *Cosmo,* too," Hanny snapped.

Sam started to pace the bedroom. "Why didn't you confront Zack? Why are you stewing and fretting when you can get it out in the open and deal with it?"

"Why didn't you confront Sonia instead of believing that cockamamie story she handed you, Sam? Because you don't like confrontations any more than Sara and I do. If I know for sure, if there is absolutely no doubt in my mind Zack is having an affair, then I have to . . . do something about it. A divorce is so . . . so final. I don't know if I'm ready for such a drastic step."

"I wish you hadn't told me this, Hanny," Sara said, crying into her pillow. "I don't need this right now. It does explain things, though."

"The three of us are a mess," Sara whispered. She reached for the soggy pillow she'd pushed at Hanny earlier and hugged it to her chest. "How did all this happen to us? One day we're all fine, happy in love, then this whole nightmare. There has to be a black cloud hanging over us. If it was just one of us, it would be different, but it's all three of us."

Hannah moved closer to her sister for comfort. "Do you want to hear something weird? The minute I realized Cisco's house was gone, I didn't think about Zack and the affair until we came up here to put the sheets on the bed. She is so devastated. I'm so glad she has Ezra. Look, guys, I feel better. I really do. It helped to talk about it."

"I'm sleeping in here with you guys," Sam said as he rummaged in the closet for a spare comforter to lay on the floor.

Sara leaned over the side of the bed and crooked her finger at her brother. "No, no, no. You sleep at the bottom of the bed to keep our feet warm. Ezra has the heat turned so low we're going to freeze."

It was exactly what Sam did *not* want to hear. The truth was, he didn't even want to be there, but they'd been inseparable from the moment they'd learned to walk. He knew in his heart it would always be that way unless he had the guts to change things. Maybe that was what their problem was. Separation anxiety. Being married was a completely different lifestyle, one they obviously hadn't adjusted to. He voiced the thought aloud, and followed up with, "God,

I love her so much."

"Well you must have done something wrong," Hard-Hearted Hannah snapped.

"Yeah, like you two did something wrong that drove your husbands to have affairs," Sam snapped back.

Hannah stretched out her legs and kicked him off the bed.

They went at it then, the way they always did, until they could make things right, at least in their own minds.

When they finally calmed down, Hannah looked at her sister and brother before she turned off the light. "Not a word of this to Cisco, okay?" Her siblings nodded. "Okay. Night, sleep tight."

"You're a sadist," Sam said as he tried to get comfortable at the foot of the bed. "My life is in ruins, and you tell me to sleep tight. You both know damn well we aren't going to sleep, so why are we doing this? Let's go downstairs and get something to eat. I'll fry the eggs, and you can make the cocoa, Sara. What do you say?"

"Best offer I've had all day. Now that you mention it, I didn't eat today. I meant to get a hot dog but got sidetracked. Come on, Hanny, hustle."

Hannah hustled. Life was suddenly looking just a tad brighter.

■ ■ ■ ■

Cisco sat up in bed when she heard the Trips tiptoeing down the hallway. She got up to let Freddie out. She debated following the dog downstairs but decided not to. Something was up with her beloved Trips. Something they didn't want her to know about. She wasn't sure, but she suspected it was serious. She would wait. If they needed her, they wouldn't be shy about asking for her help.

She turned off the light and folded her pillow under her head. Now, there in the darkness, with Ezra sound asleep, she could cry for her loss.

CHAPTER THREE

Dr. Zack Kelly was relieved when he entered the doctors' lounge to see that it was empty. A half-full pot of coffee sat on the burner. It looked black as coal. He had no doubt in his mind that it would be thick as mud. He passed it up, as well as the dried-out sugar donuts. A glance at his watch told him it was 9:50 P.M.

It was supposed to have been an early day. A day when he could have gone home at three-thirty. Weeks ago he'd arranged to have a fellow doctor take over his afternoon and early evening shift so he could take his wife out for a romantic dinner and possibly a movie. It was time to make peace with Hannah and confess to buying the boat. But ten o'clock this morning, Hanny had called and said she was going with Sam and Sara to New Jersey to visit their mother's grave. There was no way he wanted to interfere with that trip, so he said nothing about his plans for the evening. Then at noon, things had gone awry, with a bad car accident on the interstate, in which one of the passengers in the four-car pileup suffered trauma to both his eyes. After that it was a free-for-all.

At the moment he was so tired he couldn't see straight. And, he was starved. For one brief moment he debated the pros and cons of sleeping at the hospital. With Hanny gone, what was the point of going home? He heaved himself out of the comfortable chair to shrug into his down jacket. He needed to go home, even if the house was empty.

The door opened just as he was about to reach for the knob. "Well, howdy, pardner," he drawled.

Dr. Joel Wineberg grimaced as he bent down to take off his pointy-toed cowboy boots. His ten-gallon hat sailed across the room with his neckerchief. Joel always dressed up for his patients. It was probably one of the reasons he was so popular with the youngsters, and their parents as well. "I was Darth Vader yesterday. What the hell are you still doing here, Zack? I thought this was your early day. All those kids in that accident are going to make it. Thank God."

"Yeah, well, you know what they say about the best-laid plans of mice and men. We had the same emergency you did around noon, and it was downhill all the way after that. I am bushed. Wanna grab a pizza and beer at Molino's?"

"I'm your man. I think I had a muffin this morning and a lollipop around three. I'm in no hurry to go home. I'll follow you. Do you have any idea what triggered the Trips' visit to New Jersey? Kind of spur-of-the-moment if you want my opinion. Do you think they're up to something?"

Zack leered at his friend. "You mean are they harboring a deep, dark secret like we are, and they went to New Jersey to buy guns so they could shoot us both. Yeah."

Joel grimaced as he picked up his ten-gallon hat and plopped it on his head.

Fifteen minutes later both men slid into a booth at the popular watering hole all the doctors and nurses frequented after-hours. It was almost empty, though. Within seconds they gave their order to a tired waitress, who just wanted to go home. "A large pizza with the works, skip the anchovies, and two Bud Lites," Zack said.

Joel stared across the booth at his friend. "Did Hanny call?"

"If you want to call it that. She left a message around ten. I tried calling her back, but her cell phone must be off. I don't even know where they're staying. Do you?"

"At least you got a call. Sara didn't call *me,* she called my nurse and she left a message with *her.* I checked the messages at home, too."

Zack's voice sounded lame when he said, "I guess they're too busy for chitchat."

Joel's eyes popped at Zack's words. "You mean busy like we're busy or wanting to appear busy in order to make a point."

"Take your pick." Zack reached for the Bud and guzzled half of it in one gulp. Joel did the same thing. "I might have four more of these since I'm off tomorrow. Really off. It took me weeks to convince Stevens to take over for me. I promised him Knicks tickets for this weekend. I was going to surprise Hanny.

"Hell, I never even got a chance to tell her." He guzzled the remainder of the beer and thumped the red, Formica-topped table for another. Joel did the same thing.

"I'm off, too. What are we going to do, Zack?"

"Nurse our hangovers and complain to each other about what jerks we are. We are, you know. What did those two wonderful girls see in us, Joel?"

"We're good-lookin'. We're successful doctors. The possibility looms out there that one day we may discover a cure for something. We're caring individuals. And we clean up good.

"Oh, yeah, we're sneaky, and we told a few little fibs to our wives. Did I forget anything?"

"If we're such hot stuff, how come you and I are sitting here swigging beer and waiting for pizza while our wives go to New York to *shop.* Shop my ass. They used that excuse about going to the cemetery because it sounded good. They're going shopping. Those triplets are up to something. I know it as sure as I'm sitting here. I bet you they're talking to some fancy New York lawyer who charges seven hundred dollars an hour about divorcing us." Zack thumped his bottle on the tabletop again. Joel did the same thing. More beer arrived with the pizza.

Joel felt light-headed. The beer was going right to his head. "Oh yeah, well, I'll . . . I'll contest it. So there. Love has to count for something." He picked up a slice of pizza, chomped down, and immediately burned his tongue. He dropped the pizza, the topping sliding down his shirt. He yelped at the burning sensation on his chest.

"Stop being such a baby, Joel. Suck it up. I'm a doctor. When we get home, I'll put some burn ointment on it. You aren't going to die."

Joel squinted at his friend. "You are a callous bastard! How do you know I won't die? People die from burns all the time."

"I'm not happy, Joel."

"Well, guess what, Zack, I'm not happy either. We're also getting drunk, so we shouldn't be talking about something so important when we're in this condition. We should have confessed a long time ago, but you said not till we had all our certificates in hand. Well, we passed all our courses, and where are the damn certificates?"

"Shut up, Joel. Just eat the damn pizza so we can go home.

"How could you forget, Joel? I told you yesterday that Marylee called and will hand-deliver our certificates tomorrow evening. Then she called back and said she wasn't sure if the certificates would be ready or not. I already committed to dinner, so we're stuck, with or without the certificates. So we eat out again, what difference does it make? I no longer remember what a home-cooked meal tastes like." Zack heaved a sigh of frustration. "Since we are both drunk, I say we get a cab, and you bunk at my house since I live closer than you do. We *could* go to New York tomorrow."

Joel shoved half a slice of pizza into his mouth and chewed, his eyes crossed as he tried to digest what his friend said. "You go. Hanny didn't use the D word with you. Yet. I'm not stepping on Sara's toes. You think about this, you eye surgeon. What happens if the three of them gang up on us. It won't be pretty. They're tough! Remember how they beat each other up that Christmas we met them. They were bloodied and black-and-blue. And we still thought they were beautiful. I'm afraid of them," he said pitifully.

"Oh, yeah, I forgot about that. Okay, we won't go to New York. It would be a waste of time anyway since they'll be back tomorrow. We'll stay home and hatch a plan to make them *want* us."

"You must be drunk. They hate our guts! What kind of plan?" Joel asked suspiciously.

"I don't know. We have to hatch one. We'll come up with something. Trust me."

The owner of Molino's, who also doubled as the bartender, suddenly appeared at their table. "Come on, Docs, I'm driving you home. It's closing time, and I don't want you giving my place a bad name."

Zack looked up at the chubby man, then

he looked around and didn't see anyone but the tired waitress. "No one is here, Mo."

"News travels fast in the medical community, Doc. Upsy-daisy. You can pay me tomorrow. Come on now, let's do it the easy way. My wife is waiting for me."

"You hear that, Joel. This fine man's fine wife is waiting for him." He fixed his bleary gaze on Mo, and said, "I hate you."

Joel stumbled out of the booth. "Yeah, I hate you, too, because he hates you."

"Tomorrow you'll love me. Zip up those jackets, it's cold out there."

"Don't you have a heater in your car?" Joel demanded.

"Yep, I do, but you two fine, upstanding doctors are going to be sitting in the back of my pickup truck with Cleopatra."

"Who's Cleopatra?" Zack said as he tried to zip up his jacket. He failed miserably.

"My killer rottweiler. She protects me. Let's go, boys. Tessie, lock up!" Mo shouted over his shoulder as he herded his passengers out to his Ford Ranger.

"Okay, Mo."

"We're drunk, Joel," Zack hissed in his friend's ear. "We're doctors!"

"We're human beings, too. Plus, we're miserable. I can't believe we're going to ride in this rusty tin can with a dog named

Cleopatra."

"Okay, boys, up and at 'em," Mo said, giving both doctors a mighty shove. They fell forward.

"God, what *is* that smell?" Zack bellowed, just as the ninety-pound rottweiler jumped in the truck and started to nuzzle Zack's cheek. "Ah, Hanny used to do that. This dog loves me. Did you see that, Joel?"

"Shut up, Zack," Joel said as he tried to get as far away from the offensive odor as he could.

"It's manure, peat moss, and stuff from my compost heap. Breathe through your mouth, boys," Mo said.

"Your dog loves me, Mo," Zack said.

"Don't fool yourself. I told you that dog is a killer. She's just making sure you don't fall out of her watch. Don't make any sudden moves, and you'll be fine. Now, tell me where you live, and I'll have you home in no time. Cleo isn't fond of a lot of conversation either, so be quiet back there."

"It's cold back here," Joel said, as the truck whipped out of the parking lot, the wind buffeting them from side to side. "The smell is making me sick."

"Didn't you hear Mo? This dog doesn't like conversation, so stop whining." As if on cue, Cleo started to sniff Joel's leg and started to growl. Joel clamped his lips tight as Mo swung the Ranger around a curve, then blasted down the road.

"Oh, God, this dog is eating my shirt. She's going to go for my throat. Mo was right, she's a killer," Joel said as he tried to rear back away from the monster dog.

"It's the pizza on your shirt. Shut up. I want to get home in one piece. I've never been this cold in my life. Well, maybe that Christmas when we got lost in that snowstorm and the Trips found us."

Cleo growled again, this time with menace. Zack tried to wiggle between the bales of peat moss to get out of her way. He, too, clamped his lips shut.

As Mo steered the truck up and down the hills and around hairpin curves, Zack and Joel rolled from side to side. Cleo became unhappy with these goings-on. Her own stance was secure in the bed of the truck. Finally, she planted her two front legs on Joel's chest, her hind legs on Zack's stomach. Then she growled to make her point — stay still. The doctors didn't move a muscle.

When the Ranger finally came to a stop in Zack's driveway, Zack rolled over, and muttered, "I've been in some hair-raising situations in my time, but this was one of the worst."

"Shut up, Zack," was all Joel could manage with Cleo in his face.

The cab door opened and shut. "C'mere, baby," Mo said to the rottweiler. Cleo hopped out of the pickup and nuzzled Mo's leg. "You did good, little girl," he said soothingly to the big dog. "Let's go, boys, you're home." He looked around at the quiet street, the dark house, and muttered under his breath.

"What did you say?" Zack asked, falling out of the truck on his hands and knees.

"I just said it's hell coming home to a dark house. I like lights. I like to open the door and know someone who cares about me is waiting for me. Running a pub isn't easy. The hours are late, I always smell like booze and cigarette smoke, but my wife always gives me a big hug and a kiss. I have to carry a baseball bat and a gun that I have a license for so I won't get robbed. Like I said, it's tough. Guess your wife is sleeping, huh, Doc?"

"Nah, she's out of town. Doesn't your wife complain about you working such long hours at the pub?"

"In the beginning she was a little upset. But neither one of us is college-educated, so we have to make a living however we can. Teresa works at a nursery, so that takes up

73

her days. We talk on the phone ten or twelve times a day. Sometimes she brings me lunch, and we picnic behind the pub. It's give-and-take. We managed to put our four boys through college with all our hard work. Oh, yeah, one other thing, you have to talk pretty to your wife. All the time. Not just once in a while. From time to time you have to surprise her. You know, some little thing that makes her eyes light up. Something that says you're glad you married her. Anytime you boys want to talk or ask for advice, call me and set up an appointment. I'm cheaper than a shrink."

"What makes you think we need . . ."

Mo held up his hand. "Hey, I'm a bartender. I've seen it all. When two young bucks like yourselves come into my place looking like the world just caved in, I put two and two together.

"I can do that because I am as-tute!"

"Thanks for bringing us home, Mo. We'll pick up our cars tomorrow," Joel said.

"No problem. Cleo, say good night to your new friends. Bend down, gentlemen." Joel and Zack did as ordered. Cleo rose on her hind legs and wrapped her front paws around their necks and gently licked their cheeks.

"Loved by a dog!" Zack mumbled as he

made his way up the walkway to the front door, where he fumbled in his pocket for the house key. He opened the door but didn't go into the dark house. Instead, he watched Mo back up the Ranger and head down the street.

The wind whipped up again. "Feels like snow."

"That guy has it all, Zack. He's one happy man, and that dog probably loves him as much as his wife does. How many years did we go to school? Look at us! We're supposed to be smart, and, guess what, we don't have a clue about life. We have a *profession.* Will you turn on the damn light already. I'm freezing out here. I just want to go to bed."

"You sure are cranky, Joel." Zack turned on the light, closed the door, and set the alarm. He looked around the quiet house, his shoulders slumping. Joel flung his arm around his friend's shoulders.

"If it's any consolation to you, old buddy, my house is the same. Empty. Tidy and empty. Like no one lives there. That's why I didn't want to go home. We can talk in the morning when our heads are clear. Right now I just want to take a shower and hit the sheets. What the hell time is it anyway?"

"Almost two o'clock. Maybe one o'clock. Does it make a difference?"

"No. I don't even know why I asked," Joel said, heading for the stairs. "Guest room, right?"

"Yeah, second door on the right. Hanny always keeps the guest room made up in case Cisco or Ezra wants to stay over. See ya in the morning."

"Aren't you coming to bed?"

"In a few minutes."

Zack wandered through the rooms of the house, stopping to look at something, to touch something else. Everything reminded him of Hanny.

He'd been the typical young yuppie doctor when she came into his life and turned it upside down. He didn't think it was possible to fall in love at first sight, but that's exactly what had happened to him. God, how he loved her. And she loved him. He was sure of it. Yet something had gone awry, and he wasn't sure how it had happened. Maybe it was him. Maybe he was giving off bad vibes. Who the hell was he kidding? It all started the day he got the idea to buy the boat. Whatever was going on was all his fault, and he had no clue how to make it better.

Zack sat down at the table and looked around. Hanny had been so happy when she decorated the kitchen. When she was finished, she'd smiled at him, and said, "It looks just like my mom's kitchen. Not that I remember it, but my dad showed me pictures of Mom baking and cooking, stuff like that."

The room was cozy and comfortable, and when he was home, which wasn't often, he liked sitting at the table with Hanny, just having coffee together or talking. Watching the early-morning news and weather.

It was all so neat and tidy, nothing out of place. Except maybe the pumpkin on the window seat because Halloween was over. Hanny liked to decorate the kitchen for every single holiday. They had shamrocks for St. Patrick's Day, Easter bunnies for Easter, flags for the Fourth of July. Sometimes she just decorated for the fun of it. It had to be a childhood thing that her grandmother instilled in her. Joel said Sara did the same thing. He wasn't sure about Sam, though.

Hanny had made this old house with the big front porch a home. Maybe, in time, she'd come to view it the way she'd viewed Cisco's house in the valley at the foot of the Allegheny Mountains.

Zack thought about his own childhood. He'd had a nice normal life, but his family hadn't been all that close. At least not close the way Hanny's was. But the closeness in the Cisco family had developed out of necessity when Hanny's mother died. And she was one of a set of triplets. The bond among the three of them was so strong nothing could ever sever it. He hadn't had that kind of relationship with his siblings. He didn't even know where his brothers were living these days. Every year or so, one or the other would make an effort to say hello. Sometimes there were Christmas cards, and other times the holidays came and went without any kind of greeting. Maybe that was one of the things that drew him to Hanny and her family. A family that welcomed him with wide-open arms.

If he were a kid, he could cry. But he wasn't a kid. He was an adult, a surgeon. A man of responsibility. He was also a husband and a human being. How, he wondered, did a mere human separate the two?

Zack cringed when he remembered the last fight he'd had with Hanny. Her words still rang in his ears. "Tell me, Zack, what kind of life do we have where our only quality time is in bed? When you get home after midnight or when you get up at five in the morning? I have no intention of spending my life in bed with you."

At first he'd laughed at the way it sounded.

Hanny's eyes had narrowed, and he quickly fell back and regrouped, but it hadn't worked. She was right, though, because that was what hurt. Because he didn't know what to do about it. That was when he should have 'fessed up about the boat, but he'd been a coward. Things snowballed after that, and it was all his fault.

Damn.

Zack took one last look around the kitchen before he turned off the light. He smiled at the yellow frog sitting on the counter, a cookie jar filled with his favorites, Fig Newtons. A matching planter, also in bright yellow, sat on the end of the window seat. A feathery green plant was draped down the side. It looked lush and healthy. Hanny was a frog fanatic. Even the yellow place mats had frogs embroidered on the corners. The hanging planters in the window were yellow with green ferns. Hanny obviously had a green thumb.

Zack's eyes were moist when he turned off the light and headed for the stairs to his room, where he would sleep alone. For the first time in his married life. Maybe he would sleep downstairs on the couch. Yeah, yeah, sleeping on the couch wouldn't be such a bad thing, and he wouldn't have to make the bed in the morning. He wouldn't have to undress either.

"I miss you, Hanny," he whispered as he punched at the pillows on the couch. Before he closed his eyes, he sniffed at the pillow. It smelled like Hanny.

The moisture in Zack's eyes trickled to the corners of his eyes and rolled down his cheeks. He didn't care.

CHAPTER FOUR

Cisco knew she was dreaming because in the dream she was a young girl running through the valley, being chased by a fat little brown-and-white puppy. When she was winded, she sat down on a fallen log and cradled the puppy to her cheek. He was so warm, so comforting, so full of love, and he was all hers.

She opened one eye and stared into the soft brown eyes of Freddie, who reared up and licked at her wrinkled cheek.

"My goodness, is it time to get up, Freddie? It feels like I just fell asleep. Good Lord, what *is* that noise?" Cisco swung her legs over the side of the bed, hating to leave the warmth of the down comforter.

Ezra was already at the window. "I think you should come over here, Loretta. This is something you need to see."

Cisco padded over to the window. "Oh, my goodness!" was all she could manage.

"The town turned out to rebuild your house. There must be two hundred people down there in the valley. Let's get dressed and go down there to see what's going on. Hurry, Loretta."

"I guess a shower can wait till later," Cisco mumbled as she walked into the large dressing room off Ezra's room to change into warm clothing. "Why are they doing my house first? What about everyone else's house?"

"Loretta, I never thought I'd live to see the day of an old-fashioned barn raising here in the Allegheny Mountains of Pennsylvania. You'd think we would have had something like that in Wyoming, but we didn't. This is an old-fashioned house raising. I don't know for certain, but I think if the weather holds today, the shell will go up, the plumbing will be in, and so will the wiring. Tomorrow, the outside crew will start on one of the other houses, and it will be like a domino effect. Father Drupieski was telling me how it worked the other day. Get all the outside work done so that heat and water can be installed along with the Sheetrock before the weather turns bad. I'm sure they did it the democratic way by picking a name out of the hat, and yours came up first. They're your friends, Loretta. This is what friends do. They're trying to repay you for everything you've done for the town."

Cisco wiped at the tears at the corners of her eyes. "It's . . . it's so wonderful. And, it's so cold. We should make coffee for the workers," she said as she made her way carefully down the hill, the dogs at her side to make sure she didn't slip or fall.

"Look over there under the sycamore, Loretta. The ladies of the town have set up a kitchen with propane stoves. Everything is taken care of. It's nice to have such warm, caring friends. It was never like this when I lived out West. I'm just glad to be a part of this little town, your friends, and your life."

Cisco squeezed his arm.

The women welcomed Cisco with hugs and gay chatter. A cup of strong, black coffee was thrust into her hands. Ezra moved off to where the men were working to offer his help.

"I don't know what to say," Cisco said tearfully.

One of Cisco's neighbors, a woman older than Cisco herself, smiled and patted her shoulder. "This is what we do here in the valley for our neighbors, you should know that better than anyone. Your role is to have a housewarming when you move into the house. Now, we could use some help with these egg sandwiches." Cisco laughed when her neighbor slipped Freddie and Hugo strips of crisp bacon.

Another neighbor said, "According to our schedule, all the houses will be up and habitable by Thanksgiving. We'll worry about shingles and paint in the spring. Our goal is to have everyone in their new house by Thanksgiving. Just pray the weather holds. With the money you've given Father Drupieski and the checks from the various insurance companies, all things are possible. We all voted to pool the insurance money since some of the homeowners received more than others."

Cisco nodded as she thought about all the funerals she'd attended in the past several days. "We are all so blessed. Thank you seems inadequate." Tears puddled in her eyes again. Someone wiped them away with the hem of an apron. *My friends.*

"It'll do," the women chorused. "I think we need more coffeepots."

"I think Ezra has several. One rather large one that makes about twenty-five cups. I'll go get them if someone will loan me her car keys."

While Cisco was concerning herself with

coffeepots and home building, Zack Kelly roused himself from the living-room sofa and made his way to the kitchen, where his friend was busy making coffee. A box of Cheerios and a bottle of milk sat in the middle of the table.

"What happened to bacon and eggs or pancakes?" Zack grumbled.

"Yeah, what about them? I do Cheerios. Take it or leave it, buddy." Joel looked like a wild man, with his hair standing on end, his clothes wrinkled and messy.

"I'll take it as soon as I brush my teeth. I think we have orange juice. At least we always used to have orange juice. Maybe that was before Hannah went on strike."

"Go brush your teeth, Zack, then we need to talk. *Really* talk."

Zack was back in less than ten minutes. "Look, it's all under control. I'm going to tell Hannah the first moment it feels right. I don't think it's going to be as bad as we've been anticipating. The girls are wonderful. We'll have all our boating certificates to prove we know what we're doing. The condos I rented in Miami will be ready for us to move into on January 1. Look, Joel, we did it, and we can't back out now. I'm more than willing to get down on my knees and do whatever I have to do to get Hannah to forgive my . . . my . . . whatever we want to call our lack of trust."

Zack stared at his friend. There couldn't be a better friend in the whole world than Joel Wineberg. Joel had taught him how to make his first slingshot. Not that either of them had ever hit anything. It was enough just to own one to show around to their buddies. He'd taught Joel how to shinny up trees. Falling out of trees was one of Joel's specialties. Over the years, two broken arms and a busted kneecap amply demonstrated that Joel needed to find a different sport.

They'd been inseparable during their school years, as well as college. Medical school had been a challenge for both of them. Somehow, they'd never had a fight, but one would readily fight anyone else if necessary to secure the well-being of the other. They had a mutual respect that had never been called into question until now. He felt a tad guilty that he had convinced Joel to go in on the boat deal. Not that he'd had to do much convincing. Still, he felt guilty.

"I was all set to tell Hannah this weekend. Man, you don't know what I had to do to get the time off, and, what happens, my wife blows me off for a shopping trip to New York."

Joel fiddled with his Cheerios, filling up the spoon, then dumping them back in the milk.

"How about dinner this evening even if Marylee and Corinne cancel out? My treat since I didn't provide a decent breakfast for you, buddy."

"Yeah, okay. Dinner, but call and confirm. Pick me up around seven, so I can get my car from Mo's. I don't think we paid our bill last night either. Call me a cab, okay?"

Zack obliged.

After Joel left, Zack sat at the table for a long time, roll calling the special events in his life. He tried not to think about what Hannah's reaction would be when he finally got up the nerve to tell her about the boat and the coming year. What had he been thinking when he coaxed Joel into going along with the idea? He knew he was standing on a slippery slope, and he was starting to get frightened. What if Hannah walked out on him? It would be his fault if Sara walked out on Joel. How could he handle something like that? *For a doctor, you're pretty damn stupid, Zack Kelly. You only thought about yourself. You aren't single anymore, and those old rules don't count. Why did you assume your dream would be Hannah's dream, too? Why?*

Zack reached across the table and picked up Joel's bowl of soggy cereal. His face crunched up into a look of pain as he pitched it toward the back door. He watched cereal and milk splatter the door, the curtain, and the floor. He didn't feel one damn bit better, and now he had a mess to clean up.

Instead of doing that, Zack headed for the bedroom, where he changed into a sweat suit and sneakers. A minute later, he was out of the house and ready to run his ten miles, something he tried to do at least three times a week. Outside, he was surprised at how cold it was. Not that it mattered. When he got back, he would take a shower, build a fire, and sit and think.

As Zack started his ten-mile run, the Trips were on their way to New Jersey via New York, where they had spent the night at the family's apartment at the Dakota, the historic building on Manhattan's Upper West Side, because Hannah had said she wanted to buy some special yarn.

"I just want to know one thing," Sara said. "Why are we doing this? Going to the cemetery to talk to Mom isn't going to change anything if our husbands are having affairs. Sam isn't sure about Sonia, so to me this whole thing is stupid. We've already been gone for an entire day. I say we just go back home and deal with this problem like the adults we're supposed to be," Sara said.

"I'm all for that. Whose idea was it to make this trip in the first place?" Hannah demanded. Both of them turned to look at Sam, who clenched his teeth and told them to shut up.

He spotted the overhead sign a half mile up the highway. He put on his signal light and moved to the right lane, where he went down the exit ramp to follow the signs. "We're going to the cemetery, so shut up. We came this far, and I'm not going back till I talk to Mom. You, you, it's all about you! Don't you get it, we *need* to talk to Mom."

There was relief in Hannah's voice when she said, "You're right, Sam, but let's stop and get a Christmas grave blanket. The YMCA sells them, or at least they did last year. It's on the way, Sam."

"Good idea," he said. "A really big one with a red bow and some holly. Mom loved big red bows. Do you guys remember how our Christmas presents always had those red shiny, feel-good bows on them? Sometimes the bows were bigger than the present. Cisco says there's something about red bows that makes presents special."

"Yeah, yeah, Cisco always says that," Sara mumbled as she struggled with what she was going to share with her mother.

"We aren't going to find any answers at the cemetery, you all realize that, right?" Hannah said.

"So what?" Sam barked. "I always feel better after I leave."

"We do, too," Sara and Hannah said together.

"We should be solving our own problems now. We are adults, believe it or not. I'm not expecting answers. I just want to . . . to . . . *unload.* I like to believe Mom understands, and maybe one of these times she'll show me a sign or something. Her spirit. You read about things like that all the time," Sara said.

"You were right," Sam said. "The YMCA is selling Christmas trees and grave blankets. Okay, pony up, we split it three ways. That way Mom knows it's from all of us. The sign says they're a hundred bucks." The girls dived into their purses while Sam rummaged in his wallet. He was back in five minutes with a fragrant balsam grave blanket. The heady scent immediately filled the truck.

Ten minutes later they were at the cemetery. Sam carried the evergreen blanket with the huge red bow. They ran down the path shouting, "We're here, Mom!"

They cried as they dropped to their knees on the cold, frozen ground because they always cried when they visited their mother. Then they whispered the way they always did to their mother, one-on-one.

They always rose at the exact same time, looked at one another with wet eyes, touched the stone, then waved good-bye. In unison they called out, "We'll be back."

They would always go back, forever and ever. After all, it was their Mom who was resting here.

An hour later, the triplets were back in the truck, riding in silence, an unusual occurrence for the three of them. Sam broke the silence. "It's times like this when I miss having a mother," Sam said. "Mothers know everything. They always have the right answers."

Sara leaned across the seat to pat her brother's shoulder. "Cisco was a perfect stand-in. I don't think our mom could have done a better job of raising us than Cisco did. She was always there for us, every step of the way. She still is."

"I know that, Sara. But a mom is a mom.

No one can ever take her place. A person can stand in for a mom but can never take her place. Cisco told us that a hundred times. Sometimes I just want to yell, 'Hey, Mom!' and have her answer me. Just sometimes, Sara."

"Me too, Sam. Me too. I know Hanny feels the same way," Sara said, speaking for her sister, who was busy staring out the window and not paying attention to the conversation.

It was a little past noon when Sara suggested they stop somewhere for lunch. Sam drove until he saw the next exit and pulled off.

It was a simple lunch, BLTs, the bacon crisp, the lettuce crispier, the tomatoes just right, french fries and soda pop. "You two go ahead and eat; I'm going to call Joel," Sara said. "I meant to do it earlier, but, Hanny . . . I just didn't do it. Not that it makes a difference — he won't be home, and I'll just get the voice mail or his pager."

Sam eyed the sandwich, then his sisters, who didn't look like they were the least bit interested in the food sitting in front of them. Suddenly, he didn't feel like eating. The truth was, he didn't feel like doing much of anything.

"Sam," Hannah said, "I'm not hungry, and I don't really feel well. I'm going out to the truck and take a nap. You and Sara finish your lunch. And don't wake me up when you get back to the truck. Okay?"

"Fine, Hanny." After Hannah left, Sam moved around the food on his plate and tried to appear as if he wasn't listening as Sara called her husband. He flinched when he heard her leave a message on their home voice mail. He continued to listen as she called Joel's cell phone and left a second message. He wasn't surprised that she didn't leave her cell phone number or the number of the phone in his truck. Translated it meant, don't call me, I'll call you. He felt as sorry for his sister as he felt for himself.

"I told you," Sara said bitterly. "He wasn't home. He never answers his cell phone. I don't know why he even has one. The only thing he answers is his pager. Can you imagine if I was in some kind of predicament and needed to get hold of him? I'm last on his speed dial. Did you know that, Sam?"

"No, Sara, I didn't know that."

"Well, I am, and I'm damn sick and tired of it. If things don't change real quick when I get back, I'm going to be making some serious decisions. I need to think . . . to deal with what Hannah said about him having an affair. I don't want to believe that, I just don't. Unfortunately, it all makes sense now.

"I'm not really hungry, Sam. You know what, I'm going to call Cisco. I . . . I need to talk to her."

"Good. I've been wanting to talk to her all day. Let's call Dad, too."

Sara whipped out her cell phone again and started punching in numbers. Ezra's number rang and rang. After the fifteenth ring, Sara hung up. "I wish Ezra would consider getting an answering machine, but he refuses, just the way he refuses to carry a cell phone. Okay, let's try Dad."

To Sara's surprise, Jonathan Cisco answered on the first ring, almost as though he were waiting for Sara to call.

"Hi, Dad, it's Sara. I just called to see how everything is going."

"Well, young lady, you three couldn't have picked a worse time to leave town. With a disaster like this, we need all the help we can get."

How chilly his voice sounded, how accusing. Sara bristled. "Look, Dad, we all did our share. We found housing and transportation for everyone affected by the tornado. We worked around the clock. We even made sure everyone had enough groceries to last them a week. We did the paperwork and followed through. It was Cisco's decision to close the office and the factory. That left us free to . . . never mind. As a matter of fact, we're on our way home as we speak."

Her father's voice became even more chilly. "The town turned out to start the rebuilding. Your grandmother's house is now up. Everyone was there to pitch in, with the exception of you three. They're working in shifts and around the clock. The valley is lit up like a stadium. I just came home to get some warmer clothes. Is there anything else, Sara?"

Sara's voice matched her father's in chilliness. "No. Tell Cisco we've been trying to call her."

"By the way, it would have been nice if your husbands and Sam's wife had made an appearance. Sonia, you, and Hannah could have helped the women. You are not making a good impression on the town. Shopping in New York is not a valid excuse for your absence or the absence of your spouses. I have to go now, Sara."

Sara screwed up her face so she wouldn't cry. She took a deep breath before she repeated the conversation to her brother. "That's one of the many reasons why I rarely call him, Sam."

"Give me a break!" Sam barked. "Don't let him get under your skin, Sara. Tell me something. Dad screws up, and we're the ones who feel guilty. What's wrong with this picture? Oh, yeah, he was full of remorse. Why, then, aren't things the way they used to be between us and our father? Were our expectations too high? Aren't we, meaning the three of us, still the same people? Dad slammed Cisco into an assisted-living facility when she broke her arm and was blind with cataracts. We took care of her and got her out of there. He screwed up with that gold digger he was going to marry. We got him to come to his senses. That means we're the good guys. It doesn't necessarily follow that he's the bad guy, but he should have shaped up by now. Why hasn't he?"

Sara sighed wearily. "Because we're all equal partners in the business even though Cisco still calls the shots. She hasn't quite forgiven him. In Cisco's eyes, Dad hasn't redeemed himself. Yet. Dad wants to be in charge. It's all I can think of, Sam. Listen, why don't you try calling Sonia again. Or better yet, leave a message on your home machine, and maybe she'll call in and hear it. You have to do something, Sam. You can't just let her go without putting up a fight."

Sam fished a cold french fry from the

plate, took a bite, made a face. "Yuk. Yes, I can let her go without a fight, Sara. I'm not being a fool here. I shouldn't have to fight for someone I love. She knows my feelings since I was never shy about expressing them. Sonia's the one with the problem. She's the one who said she could adjust to small-town living. I believed her since she grew up on a farm out in the country. I never denied her a thing. The only thing we ever disagreed on was when to start a family. She wants children right now, and I want to wait a year or so. We need time together before our lives change, and they *will* change once babies come along. Sonia wants kids right away. I was not okay with that. It was the *only* thing we couldn't agree on. Unlike your husband, I was home for dinner every night, and if she didn't want to cook, we went out. I'm not calling her, and that's final."

Sara stared at her brother. Sam was rarely vehement about anything, but he sure was now. "Okay, if you can live with your decision, it's all right with me. She does love you, Sam. I know because she told me so. You know, at one of those girl lunches where you let your hair down and share a secret or two. We shared."

Sam scoffed. "Are you telling me Sonia

has secrets? I find *that* hard to believe. If anyone is an open book, it's Sonia."

"One," Sara said curtly.

"I suppose you aren't going to tell me, is that what you're saying? I hate it when you do that, Sara. If you know something, tell me. You want me to beg, is that it?"

"Sam, I would never, ever divulge a secret if you or Hanny or some member of my blood family confided in me. We're blood, you know. Sonia belongs to our family, through marriage, so I can tell you if you really want to know. I should have told you the other day, and I'm sorry I didn't. Sonia is pregnant. Knowing your feelings, I assume she thought it better to leave. That other stuff she was telling you about why she was leaving was just . . . just to throw you off the track."

Sam stared at his sister for a full minute, his expression cold and hard before he got up, put on his jacket, and left the roadside cafe. Sara slumped even farther down into the captain's chair and started to cry.

What is happening to my family?

CHAPTER FIVE

Sara was jittery and tight-lipped, while Sam was outright surly and hateful as they continued homeward.

"I can't wait to get home. Nothing is going right for us. Nothing," Hannah said. "If you step on the gas, we can be home in time for dinner. I'm really sorry about this wasted day. I just can't seem to think clearly anymore." Sara and Sam remained mute. The rest of the trip home was made in total silence.

Hannah was right, Sam thought, when he slid his key into the lock of his empty house, *we made it home in time for dinner.* If there was anything worse than coming home to a cold, dark, empty house, he didn't know what it was. He dropped his bag by the front door and proceeded to march through the rooms, adjusting the thermostat and turning on all the lights. He carried in a pile of wood from the backyard and made a fire before he slid a chicken potpie in the oven. Then he headed upstairs, where he stripped down and headed for the shower.

Ten minutes later, he pulled on a warm-up suit and went back downstairs. He tried his best not to look at the phone, but in the end he picked it up to see if his voice mail was beeping. It wasn't. His shoulders slumped. His sigh was mighty as he headed for the kitchen and a lonely dinner.

Surprisingly, he was hungry, and he wolfed down Cisco's homemade potpie in minutes. Sonia could make potpies, too, and they were almost as good as Cisco's. Where was she? Had she returned to the other side of the world and her parents? He knew that her parents would welcome her and the child she carried with open arms. Rage ran through Sam as the words "baby" and "pregnancy" ricocheted inside his brain. How could Sonia do something so underhanded, so sneaky? How? Well, she wasn't going to get away with it. No damn way was he going to let her get away with something like this.

Sam looked around. How neat and tidy the house was. Dusty, maybe, but when Sonia was home there had never been a speck of dust anywhere. He missed her terribly. He likened the feeling to what he'd felt at the hospital when Cisco was having her eye operation.

Obviously, Sonia wasn't the sweet, gentle, young woman he'd fallen in love with. Somewhere along the way, she had turned calculating and manipulative. She wanted a baby, and she got one. Did she care that they agreed to wait a year or two to make that happen? No, she did not. Then she lied to him, after which she dumped him and ran. He wondered if she'd cleaned out their bank account. He ran down the hall to his small office. He ripped and gouged at the contents of his desk drawer in his search for their checkbook. He felt lower than a snake's belly when he saw that there were no withdrawals. Where could Sonia go with no money? Maybe she did hit the account and it hadn't shown up yet. He went online to access his account. The numbers were the same. Sonia hadn't taken a penny. What the hell did that mean?

He rifled through the mail until he came to their Visa card bill. Cash advances would give her money if she needed it. His tired eyes scanned the list of charges. They were all his. Sonia didn't believe in charging things. She liked to pay cash for the few purchases she made. He'd always thought of her as thrifty, just like him. Maybe she'd sold her jewelry. Not that she had much, but Cisco had given her a valuable strand of pearls, and his father had given her diamond earrings. He himself had given her a diamond bracelet for her birthday.

Sam took the steps two at a time, racing into their bedroom, where Sonia's jewelry box, a gift from Sara, sat on the dresser. The pearls, the earrings, and the bracelet were still there.

Sam lashed out and kicked the dresser. A yowl of pain escaped his lips as he hobbled over to the bed. He flopped down. *What is wrong with this picture?*

Sam had a deep fear that he had never talked about to anyone. He'd tried a thousand times to figure out where that particular anxiety had come from. He still didn't know.

He lived in a world surrounded by women. Maybe that was it. At times he thought he'd been brainwashed. Other times he thought he was too smart to be brainwashed, but Sara and Hanny could be insidious. They were into all kinds of psychobabble — just for fun they said — that he didn't even pretend to understand. Nor did he want to understand such female craziness.

Who the hell am I kidding? The man who

understands women hasn't been born yet.

He longed for a best friend, a buddy, someone to confide in, someone to shoot the breeze with, go to ball games with, have a beer with, but there was no one. Growing up in the valley, and being one of a set of triplets, Sam hadn't needed to establish strong friendships. Hannah and Sara were his best friends. It was that way all through school, and even college. They'd lived in the same dorm and, after the first year, they had shared an apartment. There had been a tacit agreement between the three of them that they really didn't need anyone else in any deep, meaningful way. For the most part, that was true. Siblings didn't turn on you, betray you. Siblings were loyal, and they loved unconditionally. It always came down to family. Until now, it had always been enough.

Who to talk to? Zack or Joel? He scratched that thought as soon as it entered his head. That would be the worst kind of betrayal. His father? He snorted at that thought, too. Cisco? No, not Cisco. Cisco would kick his ass all the way to the New York state line for letting Sonia get away from him. Ezra? As nice and as wonderful as Ezra was, he couldn't see himself unloading to the older man. There were some strained feelings between Erza and his own children they weren't privy to. No, not Ezra. Then who?

The answer was right in front of him just the way it always was — Hanny and Sara. It shouldn't be like this.

Sam looked down at his untied sneakers. He tied the laces. He was dressed for running, so run he would, even though he'd just eaten. So what if he cramped up. So what!

Sara lived a mile and a quarter away, Hanny less than a mile. If he ran at top speed, he could be at either house within minutes. Which one? He'd have to play it by ear. If Zack was home, he'd go to Sara's. If Joel was home, he'd return home and go to bed. The decision made, he picked up his wallet and keys and left the house.

Sam's legs pumped furiously as he ran down the street, turned the corner, and headed in the direction of Hannah's sprawling ranch house. Twelve minutes later, his speed slowed as he approached Andover Street, where Hannah and Zack lived. Only one car, Hannah's, sat in the driveway. The house was lit up from top to bottom. Even the sensor lights on the peaks of the house glowed. He knew that Hanny had always been afraid of the dark. He was surprised that she still was. On the other hand, maybe it was a welcome home signal for Zack. Hell, maybe Hannah had a thing with the power company and agreed to burn lights for a reduction on her bill. It was such a stupid thought, he laughed out loud.

Sam walked around to the back of the house, to the kitchen, where he knocked on the door. He could see his sister at the chopping block dicing vegetables. She looked up, a smile on her face. A smile that vanished when she saw it was Sam at the door and not Zack. She motioned for him to come in.

Sam eyed the wicked-looking chopping knife as he sat down on a stool across from his sister. "What are you making? I had one of Cisco's potpies."

"Stew. In a pressure cooker so it will be ready when Zack gets home. I called and left a message that I was home making dinner." Hanny bit down on her lower lip. "He didn't call me back. I have a bad feeling, Sam. You know, like something's wrong, but you can't quite put your finger on it. Waiting for the other shoe to drop, that kind of thing. I'm thinking if I press this or accuse him, he'll choose the other *woman* over me. I don't think I could bear that. I'm just cooking to have something to do."

Hanny scooped up the carrots, the celery,

and the onions, and dropped them into the pressure cooker. She locked it, washed her hands, then sat down across from her brother and looked at him with worried eyes.

"I have a pie in the oven. One of those frozen ones. It's called Razzleberry. It's almost done."

His sister seemed so brittle all of a sudden. He really thought that if he snapped his fingers, she'd break in two. He turned off the thought. "Shut up, Hanny. I didn't come over here for a culinary dissertation. Has it ever occurred to you that neither you, Sara, nor I has a best friend? Don't look at me like that. Has it?"

Hannah tugged at her earlobe as she squirmed on the stool she was sitting on. "Is this some kind of trick question? Does it have something to do with Sonia?"

Sam swiped his hands through the tight curls on his head, his expression surly. "Will you just answer the question, Hanny?"

Hannah shrugged. "You and Sara are my best friends. You already know that, Sam, so why are you deviling me like this? Plus, you look like some kind of wild person. What's wrong?"

She looks even more brittle, as though she's crumbling from the inside now, Sam thought.

"I'll tell you what's wrong. Sara told me Sonia is pregnant. I'm her husband, and I didn't know. Do you know why, Hanny? Because I thought Sonia and I had an understanding that we would wait a few years before we started a family. Actually, it was a promise we made to each other. Sonia didn't choose to honor that promise. Now she's gone. She didn't take any money from our joint accounts. She didn't take her jewelry. I suppose it's possible her parents sent her money. Hell, for all I know she could have been saving aluminum cans and turned them in for a windfall."

"And your point is . . ."

"My point is I don't have a friend to talk to about this. A guy friend. I should have a guy friend. You should have girlfriends, and so should Sara, but you don't. None of us has friends. Think about it, Hanny. We stepped into marriages poorly prepared to be close to anyone outside our immediate family. None of us is coping. We're a damn mess is what we are."

Hannah bristled. "Speak for yourself, Sam."

"No. Listen to me, Hannah. Think about this. When you first thought that Zack was having an affair, did you tell anyone? No, because there was no one to tell but Sara or me, and you didn't want us to know. And you didn't confide in us about your suspicions until you'd worried yourself sick. If you had a best friend, I bet you ten dollars you would have told her right away. Now, you have another problem. I'm almost certain you're wrong about those two guys. How are you going to explain all this to Zack? You didn't trust him enough to find out the truth before assuming the worst about him. Face it, the three of us don't know how to interact with other people in close relationships. We're like islands unto ourselves. Even I know that's not good. When we go back for our college reunions, who are we going to be anxious to see? Which friends? We don't have any truly close friends to be concerned about. Am I getting through to you, Hanny?"

"I'll deal with it, Sam. As for friends, if you feel the need to make new ones, go out there and do it. This is all about Sonia in some cockamamie way, isn't it?" Not bothering to wait for a response, Hanny rushed on. "You take care of your problems, and I'll take care of mine. From here on in, sharing is out. Are you okay with that? By the way, did you call Cisco when you got home?"

"No. Did you?"

Hanny looked away. "No," she mumbled. "I guess what you're saying is, we're all messed up."

"Yeah. Yeah, we are, Hanny. Maybe it's not too late to get on track. One more time, if it came down to Zack or me and Sara, who would you choose?"

Hannah burst into tears. She hopped off the stool when the oven timer went off. Sam watched as she took the berry pie out of the oven and set it on a trivet. "Okay, okay, you and Sara. Now are you happy that you made me admit it? Well, are you?" she screeched.

Sam stood up, squared his shoulders, and said coldly, "That, Hannah Cisco Kelly, was the *wrong* answer. And if you think for one minute that Zack doesn't know the answer, then you are nuts. And that makes you a bigger fool than I am. Good night, Hanny."

Outside in the star-filled night, Sam hitched up his sweatpants and headed off to Sara's house. He was almost there; in another ten minutes he'd ruin her night just the way he'd ruined Hannah's.

Sam was breathing a little harder by the time he reached Sara's house. Like Hannah's, the split-level house was lit from top to bottom. Only Sara's car sat in the driveway, which meant Joel wasn't home. Once again, he made his way to the back door, expecting to see Sara in the kitchen. He peered through the half pane but the kitchen, while lit up, was empty. He rang the bell and waited. When his sister appeared he noticed that her curly hair was wet, and she was dressed in an old bathrobe. She held a glass of wine in her hand. Sam wasn't sure, but from the look in her eyes, she'd had a few glasses prior to his visit. Another unhappy camper. He waited for her to unlock the door.

"What brings you out here, Sam? Didn't you just drop me off a little while ago? Is something wrong?"

"Make some coffee and dump that wine. You look like you already have a snoot full. I'm here to ask you some questions."

Sara carried her wineglass to the sink and proceeded to make coffee. "I don't know any more than I already told you about Sonia, Sam. It's your problem, and you have to make it right. Right now I'm trying to deal with what Hanny told me about Joel."

"Look at me, Sara. Why don't you, Hanny, and I have any best friends?"

To her credit, Sara looked stunned at the question. "What are you talking about? You and Hanny are my best friends. What's with you anyway?"

"Don't you think that's a little strange,

Sara? There's a whole world out there," Sam said, motioning to the door. "A whole world with millions of people in it, and we can't call any of them our best friends. That's pretty damn sad if you want my opinion."

"Is this some sort of guy thing? It's kind of late for a talk about our lack of friends, isn't it? It's time to go to bed, Sam. Can we talk about this tomorrow?"

"No, we can't talk about this tomorrow. When Mom was alive, we played with other kids. She was always taking us to some kid's house or fetching them to our house. Not the three of us together to one house because we each had different friends. I used to play with Billy Rutherford. He lived far enough away that Mom had to drive me. You and Hanny never came with us. You had other friends. That all stopped when Mom died. What I'm trying to say here is she knew we were individuals. She didn't want us glued to each other because we're triplets, but that's exactly what happened. Let me put it to you another way, Sara. We're screwed up."

Sara turned thoughtful. "I vaguely remember a little girl named Becky. She had long braids and always had scabs on her knees. Her mom made gingerbread cookies and let us decorate them. I wonder what happened to her."

"You could always find out if you wanted to. Unless she left the valley. Cisco would know. At some point, I'm going to search out Billy. I remember one of Hanny's friends, too. Her name was Leslie Byrnes."

"Where are you going with this, Sam?"

"I don't know, Sara. Tell me something before I leave. If Joel walked in the door this minute, and I said, take your pick, him or me, who would you choose?"

Unlike Hanny, Sara didn't hesitate. She didn't bite down on her lip, didn't screech at him. The one word sailed off her lips as though it was perched there just waiting to be uttered. "You."

"*Wrong* answer, Sara." Sam's shoulders slumped as he made his way to the back door. He had his hand on the knob when Sara stopped him in his tracks.

"And if the situation were reversed, and I said, Sonia or me and Hanny, who would you choose?"

Sam's shoulders slumped even further. "Sonia," he said, closing the door quietly behind him. He pretended not to hear Sara's anguished cry as he started down the path leading to the street. He knew she would call Hanny the moment she got her

112

wits about her. He wished he had someone to call.

Sam shivered inside his sweatshirt. He'd have to run at a high rate of speed to get warm again. *Damn, I am so tired.* The dark night had turned cold, but the stars sprinkled the darkness lighting his way. Over his shoulder he could see a thin slice of the moon. He remembered a nursery rhyme about a cow jumping over the moon. He laughed then, but it was not a happy sound.

In order to keep warm, Sam picked up his brisk walking pace, then broke into a full run. He was whizzing down the street where Hanny lived when he saw Zack's BMW pull into the driveway. Just in time to eat Hanny's stew and Razzleberry pie. He wondered if Hanny would hang up the phone when Zack entered the house. Probably not. Sara was too important to Hanny.

Sam remembered Billy Rutherford very well. As he ran, finding Billy Rutherford seemed like the most important thing in the world to Sam.

Zack Kelly pressed the button on his key chain that would lock his car. He looked up at the house that he and Hannah had bought. It was all lit up. Hannah had a thing about lights. Even when the sun was out, she'd turn lights on. She was home, that was the big thing. He probably should have returned her earlier call, but he hadn't.

Suddenly, he didn't want to go into the house. While he wanted to see his wife, he didn't want to see her. The crazy thought made sense to him. He knew what he had to do, and he dreaded it. The fact that his wife was home worried him. Now he was going to have to switch gears. He needed more time, time to psych himself for the moment when he would blurt out the truth of what he and Joel had done. This definitely was not the time.

Zack looked down at his watch. Ten minutes to ten. A hell of a time to be coming home from work. Joel had canceled dinner, as had Marylee and Corinne. He thought about the egg salad sandwich he'd had for dinner, which was now lying like a lead weight in his stomach. The gallon of black coffee he'd consumed had him wired for flight.

With no dog or cat to alert Hanny to his arrival, Zack stood at the back door and watched his wife talk on the phone. She was probably talking to Sara or Sam. A daily if not an hourly occurrence. It had never bothered him before, but this time it set his teeth on edge.

He saw the pie, the pressure cooker. Hannah had made dinner. A dinner he wasn't going to eat. He watched as his wife dabbed at her eyes, which had to mean she had either been crying or was crying now. *Why?*

Suddenly he felt like a spy. He didn't like the feeling. He gave his own eyes a quick swipe before he opened the door. Startled, Hannah turned around, her face lighting up, tears sparkling in her eyes. "I'll talk to you tomorrow," she said into the phone before she hung it up. "I'm home!" she said happily, her arms extended as she walked toward him. She stopped in her tracks, her arms dropping to her sides when she noticed the cold, angry expression on her husband's face.

Zack gritted his teeth. "So I see," he said coldly. "I'm tired. I'm going to bed. I hope you had a good shopping trip." His thoughts were bitter as he recalled his wasted time off and what he'd had to do to get it.

"But, honey, I made your favorite dinner. It won't taste the same tomorrow. Can I get you a glass of wine?"

"I don't want any wine, and didn't you hear me? I'm tired, and I'm going to bed. In case you don't already know this, I've been working around the clock while you and your sister and brother were *shopping*."

Tired and not hungry had to mean he'd been with *her*. The thought sent shivers up her spine. Hannah's back stiffened. "You don't have to sound so ugly about it, Zack. You're never home anyway, so I don't think you could have missed me all that much. We all did our share before we left. I'm referring to the tornado. I also made you seven dinners and put them in the freezer, so I didn't leave you bereft. I didn't say a word when you went to that ten-day conference in California or that five-day symposium in Puerto Rico. I guess shopping is a sinful thing to do. I'm sorry. Maybe you *should* go to bed before one of us says something we'll regret. I'll eat by myself."

She looked so pretty, Zack thought. Was it his imagination, or had his wife lost a few pounds on her shopping trip? It was hard to tell with the baggy slacks and colorful reindeer sweater she was wearing. Her face did look thinner to him, though. God, how he loved her. This was going to be harder than he thought it would be. He knew in his gut she would walk out on him the minute he told her what he'd done. He steeled himself for whatever was to come next.

"Zack, we need to talk. Obviously, you're angry. I can explain . . . at least I think I can explain if you'll just give me a few minutes. The table's set, the wine's chilled. It's been a very long time since we had dinner together. Won't you reconsider? I have something important I want to talk to you about."

Zack whirled around. "You know what, Hannah, I had something important to talk to you about, too. I practically moved the earth to get this weekend off so we could spend it together, but then you had to go to New York to *shop.* Why don't we just drop this whole thing for now? I'm not hungry. I have no desire to talk, and I'm bone tired. Don't nag me, or I'll really get ticked off."

Hannah's heart thundered in her chest. Who was this hateful-sounding person standing in front of her? Zack had never uttered a cross word to her from the day he'd met her.

"Ticked off? Is that what you said? Do you want to see ticked off, Zack? Let me show you ticked off." Before Zack could blink, the pressure cooker was unlocked and the contents dumped on the floor. The Razzleberry pie skidded across the floor. "Now, that's ticked off, *Doctor.*" Before he could blink a second time, Hannah had her jacket on and her car keys in her hand. "I'm leaving, and I'm not coming back. You don't need a wife, all you need is a housekeeper or that other woman you're seeing. Don't think I don't know all about *that!*" She slammed the door so hard the panes of glass rattled in their frames.

Zack stared at the door in stupefied amazement. His wife had just walked out on him. He looked at the mess on the floor. The stew looked delicious, the Razzleberry pie, scrumptious. He really should clean it up. He really should. Instead, he called Joel on his cell phone. He relayed the events as they had transpired. "What the hell was she talking about, Joel? What other woman?"

"She's probably on her way to our house. The tension was so high when I got home I could have sliced it with a knife. I feel like a stranger in my own house. I can talk to her if you want me to. What do you suppose she wanted to tell you that was important? Hey, maybe she's pregnant! Did you think of that?" Joel asked.

"No, I don't want you to talk to my wife. Hannah's version of something important to talk about is far different from what I would think is important. Trust me on that, and no, she isn't pregnant."

"How do you know? You're just the husband. The husband is always the last to know. Don't you know anything about women, Zack? This whole thing just isn't right. You love her, I know you do, and she loves you. Stop being such a jerk. Go find her and tell her about the boat and get it over with. I'll tell Sara. The hell with the certificates. Are you seeing another woman?" Joel asked, his voice ringing with suspicion.

"I am not being a jerk. Obviously, I don't know half as much as you know about women. I'm going to bed now because I'm tired, and I don't want to clean up this mess. And no, I'm not seeing another woman. When in the hell would I have the time to have an affair?"

"Tomorrow that mess will be twice as hard to clean up because it will be dry. I'd clean it up now, Zack. It's not like you have anything else to do at the moment." The only response Joel got was the sound of a dial tone in his ear.

Zack looked again at the mess his wife had created. He groaned as he set about cleaning it up. Two rolls of paper towels later, he was ready for the mop-and-bucket brigade. When the floor sparkled underneath his feet, he washed the dishes and put them away. The kitchen looked clean and empty. Like a room in someone else's house. Suddenly, he felt choked up.

As he made his way through the house, he realized he hadn't taken his jacket off. Hannah's hand-knitted scarf, the first one she'd ever made for him, was still around his neck. He removed it and held it to his lips. It felt warm and soft, like Hannah herself.

Zack stripped down, donned his pajamas, brushed his teeth, and crawled into bed, the scarf clutched in his hands. He bunched it into a ball and brought it to his cheek. It felt like a warm caress.

Sometimes life just wasn't fair.

CHAPTER SIX

Sam felt like a programmed robot as he prepared to leave the house. He finished his coffee, turned off the machine, emptied the Pyrex pot, checked the back door, and turned off the light. At the front door, he took his jacket off the coatrack, slapped his baseball cap on his head, opened the door, turned off the light, locked the door, and headed for his car. It was still dark out because it was five o'clock in the morning. If he'd managed to get an hour's sleep, he'd consider himself lucky, he thought irritably as he made his way to the Rover.

He drove by rote, up one street, down the other, until he got to the secondary road that would take him to the new home of Cisco Candies. Travel time: sixteen minutes.

Sam unlocked the plate-glass doors at the entrance just as he felt a presence behind him. He whirled around. "Dad!"

"You're early this morning, Sam. Glad

you're back. How was New York?" Jonathan Cisco asked cheerfully.

Sam grimaced. How could anyone be so cheerful so early in the morning? "Just the way it was the last time I was there. Aren't you early, too?"

"Actually, I'm late this morning. I've been coming in at around three-thirty to catch up on things before I head off to help the others with the rebuilding that's going on. You wouldn't believe how much there is to do for those poor people.

"Listen, now that you're here, do you think you could maybe double up and take over some of my orders? I hate to let the townspeople down. We still have two more houses to go, and the weather isn't supposed to be that good the rest of the week. I have to tell you, Sam, I think I finally found my true calling. I love what I'm doing. I love working with my hands, love watching the homeowners come out to see the progress we're making. Would you listen to me? I didn't mean to bend your ear so early in the morning. Is something wrong, son? You look terrible."

Sam ignored the question as he headed for the compact kitchen, where he started to make coffee. "What does that mean, Dad, that you found your 'true calling'?"

Jonathan Cisco stared at his son for a full minute. "I don't think it's any secret that I never really wanted to go into the candy business. It was expected of me. I did it because I had to have a steady job, what with a set of triplets and a wife to support. I always wanted to make furniture. Work with my hands. Mom thought . . . there just wasn't enough money in the furniture business back then. You do what you have to do when you have responsibilities. That kind of thing. What's wrong, son?"

Sam sat down on a stool and looked up at his father. Again, he ignored the question. "Do you remember Billy Rutherford, Dad?"

Jonathan laughed. "Your shadow? Of course I remember him.

"When you weren't eating and sleeping at his house, he was eating and sleeping at our house. You two were inseparable. How strange that you should ask. He was here last week with his wife helping out. He lives in Johnstown now. That guy worked nonstop for two solid days. He likes working with his hands, too. He's an engineer. His wife is pregnant. Pretty little thing. Your grandmother gave her some recipes. Seems she likes to cook. You should look him up. He asked about you, Sam."

Sam digested the information before he

spoke. He watched as his father poured coffee into two Styrofoam cups. "After Mom died, Billy never came around anymore. No one came around. It was just Hanny, Sara, and me."

Jonathan sat down across from his son. His eyes were full of pain. "Your grandmother . . . we both . . . we were so fearful after Margie died. We wanted to keep you three close. We put you in private school, and by the time you got home . . . look, Sam, it's a long story. You had each other. I told Mom it wasn't a good idea, that you three needed outside interests, but she said she knew best. I was so full of grief those first few years I didn't argue. All I wanted was for all of you to be safe and together because that's what I thought Margie would want. You used to cry, Sam. So did Hannah and Sara. Eventually, I guess you gave up, knowing things weren't going to change.

"I think you need to tell me what's wrong, Sam."

Sam told him, watching his father carefully as the words spilled from his lips. When he finally wound down, he said, "This is between us, Dad."

"Of course. It looks and sounds like you think your grandmother and I made a mess of things. There wasn't a book to go by,

Sam, back then. We did what we thought was best. Obviously, you think we were mistaken. Are you sure Hannah is all right? I can't conceive of Zack or Joel having an affair. I'm sure she's imagining it."

"Hannah doesn't think she's imagining it. Other than the fact that she's made herself miserable, she's fine. I stepped over the line with both Hannah and Sara last night. I have to distance myself from them emotionally. I know I have to do it to survive. Remember how you used to call us a triangle?"

Jonathan smiled, his eye on the clock hanging over the stove. "What are you going to do about Sonia, son?"

"Cisco always says when you don't know what to do about something you should do nothing. I don't know. I feel like she snookered me to get what she wanted."

"Sam, Sam, Sam. Did it ever occur to you that maybe something went awry with your . . . ah . . . birth control measures. Nothing is foolproof. It's possible. Perhaps something like that did occur, and Sonia, knowing you as well as she does, knew you'd react just the way you are, so she left rather than face you. I'm not saying that happened. I'm saying it's a possibility. You should give it some thought."

Sam glared at his father. *That,* he would digest later. His voice was sad when he said, "You and Cisco took away our independence and made us dependent on one another. Didn't either one of you see what you were doing? The three of us are emotional cripples. I needed a friend last night. I needed a friend so bad I could have bawled my eyes out. I know Hanny and Sara feel the same way. What are we supposed to do, Dad? Tell me."

Jonathan looked at the pain in his son's eyes. "Cut yourself loose. Work out your problem with your wife. Don't listen to anyone but yourself, son. That's the first step. It's going to be hard. I'm so sorry, Sam. We just weren't emotionally equipped to deal with the death of your mother. It's the best defense I can come up with. Perhaps talking with a counselor will help. You can always come to me to talk. Listen, we stop work on the houses at around seven. Would you like to get a bite to eat?"

"Sure, Dad. How about Chinese at Sum Sun."

"Sounds good, Sam. I'll meet you there at eight o'clock. You sure you don't mind taking over my job here?"

"Nah. Working will keep me busy. Less time to think. I'll see you tonight, Dad."

"I'll look forward to it, son."

Sam sat in the small kitchen for a long time after his father left. He didn't know if he felt better or worse after their talk. He was on his second cup of coffee when he looked up to see Hannah standing in the doorway. Her eyes were red, her hair mussed, and she looked like she was wearing the same khaki slacks and brown sweater she'd had on the night before. He nodded curtly. "Aren't you a little early?"

"It's hard to sleep in the backseat of your car in the A&P parking lot. I figured I might as well come to work. Why are you so early?"

This was where he was supposed to ask his sister why she'd slept in her car in the A&P parking lot. Well, he really didn't care. Obviously, she'd had a fight with Zack. "I couldn't sleep either. Dad was here earlier, and we had coffee together. If you want coffee, you'll have to make some more. See ya." Without another word, Sam walked out of the kitchen and down the hall to his office. He had a lot of work, but he also had a lot of thinking to do.

A lot.

Sam kept himself busy, but at nine o'clock it was as if a silent bell rang telling him the time. He picked up the phone and dialed the Information operator in Johnstown to ask for the telephone number of William Rutherford. The operator gave him two numbers, one for Rutherford Engineering and another number for his home address. Sam copied down the numbers and ripped the sheet of paper off the sticky pad. He could feel his heart beating trip-hammer fast. He clutched at the Post-it as if it were a lifeline.

Three minutes later, Sam was announcing himself to the switchboard operator. A booming voice came over the line. Sam grinned from ear to ear. "Yeah, Billy, it's me! Damn, I'm sorry I missed you. Dad told me you were here this past weekend. Can we get together? I can come up there, or, if you want, you can come here. It's an either/or for me."

"I need to stay home this weekend. Jeez, it's good to talk to you, Sam. We had some fun times when we were kids, didn't we?"

"Yeah, Billy, we did. Look, I'm sorry . . ."

"Sam, I understand. As a kid, I didn't, but that was then, and this is now. Why don't you come and visit this weekend. We can talk it through then. By the way, your old man is a slave driver. That's a good thing. I was really bushed after last weekend. I don't mean to cut you short, buddy, but I have a meeting I have to go to. So, we're on for this weekend, right?"

"Yeah. We're on. See you Saturday, Billy."

Sam's fist shot in the air the moment he hung up the phone. Now, if he could just find Sonia, maybe his life would level off. He looked up to see Hannah standing in the doorway. "What?" he barked.

"I wanted to talk to you about something, Sam. Sara just pulled into the parking lot. Can we go into the conference room for a few minutes? Please."

Sam stared at his sister. She looked terrible. His heart softened. "Sure."

"Thanks, Sam. I know you're busy, and I appreciate it. I'll probably be working through the night myself to catch up. Sara, too. I think that might be a good thing. You know, less time to think and be miserable."

Sam let the comment go unanswered. He was thinking about Sonia, wondering where she was. Was it possible Sara and Hanny knew where she was and were keeping it a secret?

As Sam stomped his way down the hallway, he was stunned at his attitude in regard to just about everything in his life. He likened it to having lived under a dark umbrella, an umbrella he'd just closed to allow sunshine into his life. He thought maybe it was a corny analysis, something

Hannah and Sara would laugh at should he confide in them. *Like that's really going to happen.* He snorted.

"Did you say something, Sam?" Hannah asked.

"No."

Sara, Sam thought, looked perky and put together so early in the morning in a pumpkin-colored pantsuit and matching blouse. She took one look at Hannah, and said, "What's wrong?"

Hannah's eyes filled as she recounted the evening's events. "I left and slept in the car in the A&P parking lot."

Sara reared back to better observe her disheveled sister. "That was a pretty stupid thing to do, Hanny. Don't you agree, Sam?"

Sam shrugged. He was getting real good, maybe too good, at distancing himself from his sisters and their opinions. Sara shot him a puzzled look. He shrugged again.

"If that's all that's bothering you, I have to get back to work. That little sojourn to New York put me behind. We have a million Christmas orders to fill, and Dad asked me to cover for him." He was on his feet and halfway out the door when Hannah grabbed his arm.

"Wait just a damn minute, Sam. I don't much care for your attitude right now.

130

What's your problem?"

Sam jammed his hands on his hips and glared at his sisters. "My problem is *us*. You, Sara, and me. That's my problem. Do you two know where Sonia is? I'm only going to ask you once. If you know, and you don't tell me, and I find out later that you've known all along, I will never, ever, forgive or speak to you again. Are we clear on that? Think carefully before you answer me."

Sara shuffled her feet, and Hannah looked everywhere but at Sam.

This, Sam knew by the fierce look on his sisters' faces, was one of those times where one or the other of them was going to throw a punch. He jammed his hands in his pockets, a clear sign that he didn't want any part of whatever they were contemplating. He turned, stalked his way to his office, and slammed the door. Knowing his sisters the way he did, he turned around and locked the door, then closed the vertical blind. His eyes burned, and his shoulders shook as he sat down in his swivel chair.

He'd just taken the first step on his road to independence.

Back in the conference room Sara and Hannah looked at each other in open-mouthed amazement. "What is his problem other than Sonia?" Sara asked.

"Isn't that enough?" Hannah snapped.

"Why didn't you come to my house last night? Or Sam's? You could have gone to Ezra's house, too. What's going on, Hannah? By the way, you look awful."

Hannah perched on the end of the conference room table and looked around. She'd decorated the room and was proud of it. Buyers always complimented the serenity of the room. It was just another way of saying they appreciated that Cisco Enterprises didn't do a hard sell.

All the old pictures from the New York factory had been cleaned, reframed, and now hung in chronological order, starting with Cisco's first batch of candy made in her kitchen right up through the ground breaking for the new building and the final picture of Cisco entering the new building the day it was completed.

A decorative fish tank with tropical fish swimming lazily added to the calmness of the room. The soft mint green drapes and matching carpet muted any and all sounds. A huge ficus tree underneath the skylight was tall and stately, as was the banana tree Sam had insisted on parking in one of the free corners.

The table and all twelve chairs were solid oak with yellow cushions. Along with a fresh

132

bouquet of yellow flowers that always sat in the center of the long table, the yellow cushions were her way of bringing sunshine into the room. That day's flowers were glorious, yellow and white spider mums that were big as grapefruits.

"Well," Sara prodded.

Hannah licked her lips. "I didn't think it was going to be like this. I'm more convinced than ever that Zack is having an affair. I all but accused him of it, and he didn't deny it. He said he was too tired to eat dinner last night. He was probably with her and they had . . . food and . . . sex. Why would he want my stew and Razzleberry pie? I dumped it all on the floor for him to clean up. I just blasted out of there, huffing and puffing like some deranged person. I'm not proud of it, Sara. Now I don't know what to do."

Sara fiddled with her wedding ring as she watched her sister. Normally, she would have walked over to Hanny and wrapped her arms around her. For some reason, she fought the impulse to comfort her sister. The rules seemed to have changed overnight, thanks to Sam. Now, like Hanny, she didn't know what to do.

"Cisco always said when you don't know what to do, do nothing."

Hannah bit down on her clenched fist. "What does that mean, Sara, do nothing? Does it mean don't go home? Go to a motel? What?"

Sara shrugged. "I really have to get back to work, Hannah. I'm behind on my work with the trip and all."

"Oh, so you're saying I screwed everything up. Go ahead, blame me. Everyone always blames me for everything anyway."

"That's not what I said. I said we're all behind because we took two days off. We never caught up from the week Cisco closed the factory. I didn't blame you for anything. I want to get caught up. I don't want someone else to do my work. How hard is that to understand? We get a paycheck from Cisco Candies every week. I like to earn mine. By the way, do you know where Sonia is?"

"No. If I had to take a guess, I'd say she's at the Allegheny Inn. I'm keeping my nose out of Sam's business. He's like some wild hare these days."

Sara threw her hands in the air. "See you later."

Hannah sat alone when the door closed behind her sister. She couldn't ever remember being so miserable. She hopped off the table and walked over to the fish tank. Her index finger traced one of the rare colorful fish as it swam one way, then the other. How calm and peaceful they were. No cares. No worries. Did fish even care? Probably not. Suddenly she longed for Freddie, Cisco's loyal, loving golden retriever. Freddie was so warm and comforting. But these days Freddie had a new friend in Hugo. Damn, nothing was working out right. Nothing.

Hannah sprinkled fish food into the tank before she turned off the lights and closed the door to the conference room.

Today was supposed to be a wonderful, bright new day. Instead, it was a gray day filled with guilt and doubt. And it was all her own doing.

Her shoulders squared, her head high, Hannah marched down the hall to her office. She'd decorated that room, too. She'd painted the walls yellow, her favorite color. Luscious green plants that she tended lovingly were healthy and vibrant. The wall directly in her line of vision held hundreds of framed photographs of her siblings, Cisco, her father, and, of course, Freddie. There was one picture of Zack standing under the sycamore holding a pumpkin he'd carved. The first pumpkin he'd ever carved, he'd said. That was it, one picture of Zack. Later she would think about *that*.

Hannah hunkered down and accomplished in three hours what it would have taken another employee a full day to do. When she was satisfied that she could indeed catch up in the afternoon and into the evening, if she wanted, she reached for her jacket and left the office. She was going home to shower and change and head for the hospital to talk to Zack. If she had to, she would wait all day until he appeared. She couldn't live like this one more day.

Settling things was her mission now.

CHAPTER SEVEN

Loretta Cisco stepped out of the elevator of Larkspur Community Hospital and stood for a moment to view the lobby. For some reason she hadn't paid attention to the decor when she'd arrived an hour earlier. At that point she'd been excited because she was going to be able to tell Bertha Williamson she could move into her new house the minute she got out of the hospital. Bertha had cried buckets, soaking her shoulder cast, her old hands trembling as she stared at Cisco through her tears. That particular moment made the tragedy almost bearable.

Cisco looked now with appreciation at the decorations in the lobby, compliments of the fifth-grade class of Larkspur Elementary School. Turkeys and Pilgrims were everywhere, as were colorful bronze, gold, and bright red leaves. The windows had been painted with scenes from Plymouth, amateurish but still beautiful. *Oh, to be that young again.*

As Cisco made her way to the plate-glass doors, she noticed a forlorn figure huddled in one of the blue chairs near the small café manned by volunteers. The young woman had a pile of knitting in her lap.

Cisco trundled over to the young woman. "Hannah! What are you doing here?"

Hannah looked up, a stunned expression on her face. "Cisco!"

We could be a comedy team, Cisco thought. "Is something wrong? What are you doing here, honey?"

"Oh, no. No, nothing's wrong. I'm waiting for Zack. Did you come to visit someone, Cisco?"

"Bertha Williamson. I wanted to be the first one to tell her she could move into her house the day she gets out of here. Which will be in a few days. Father Drupieski took it upon himself to gather together a small army to help Bertha around the clock until she's ready to take over herself. Everything is working out so nicely. I had my doubts there for a little while. Is Zack off today, or is he making rounds?" *She looks so . . . miserable. Even the makeup she rarely wears doesn't look right. She's lost some weight, too.* "Hannah, honey, is something wrong?"

"What could be wrong, Cisco? No. You

know me. No patience. Zack has no sense of time," she finished lamely. Her head jerked upright. "Aren't the Thanksgiving decorations precious? One of the volunteers told me the fifth-grade class painted them over the weekend. Way back when, Sam, Sara, and I wanted to be part of it, but that private school we were in didn't do stuff like this. Everyone who enters the lobby smiles. Did you ever see so many turkeys in one place?"

She's babbling, and she's so brittle she's about to snap in two, Cisco thought. Out of the corner of her eye she could see Ezra at the front entrance in his brand-new pickup truck. "I haven't seen much of you lately, Hannah. I wish you, Sam, and Sara would stop by. It gets lonely up there on the hill in Ezra's plate-glass home. They tell me I can move into my own house over the weekend. I want to make Thanksgiving dinner in my own home. I hope I can get used to a new stove." Now she was babbling, just like Hannah. She could hear the knitting needles clicking, and even from where she was standing she could see the mess her granddaughter was making with the yarn. She wondered what she was making.

"Sure, no problem; I'll stop by, Cisco."

This was where Hannah was supposed to

jump up and hug her, but she didn't. Her eyes were on the elevator. Cisco frowned as she walked closer and bent down to kiss Hannah's cheek. "I'll look forward to your visit. I miss you all."

Hannah tore her gaze away from the elevator. "What did you say, Cisco?"

"Nothing. I guess I'll see you when I see you. Tell Zack I said hello."

"Yes. Yes, I'll tell him."

Still no hug. Cisco's shoulders slumped. What in the world was wrong with this granddaughter of hers? Whatever it was, it was spreading like a virus. Sam was in some kind of a, what the young people today called, funk, and Sara was much too quiet and serious — totally unlike her usual upbeat self.

When Cisco reached the door she took a last look at her granddaughter. Hannah's knitting needles were clicking furiously, but her gaze was still on the elevator. Something was definitely wrong. For the first time in her life, Cisco felt lost. The Trips had always come to her in the past when there was a problem. Always.

Cisco's eyes burned as she stepped out into the biting November air. Ezra appeared and held her elbow as she climbed into his new Ford Ranger.

Ezra eyed the woman he loved so dearly, correctly interpreting the expression on her face. "Whatever it is, Loretta, we'll talk about it and make it right."

Cisco reached for Ezra's hand and squeezed it. She nodded because if she tried to speak, she knew she'd start to cry.

Inside the hospital, Hannah looked up when she saw a blur of white coming toward her. Alice, Zack's nurse, and her father's significant other. She felt herself cringe, then she stiffened. She struggled to smile. "Hello, Alice, what brings you down here? I thought you went off duty at three o'clock."

"Today I have to work till six. I came in three hours late because I had to get a bone density test and my yearly mammogram. Are you waiting for someone, Hannah?"

"Yes, my husband. Is he in surgery?"

Alice smiled brightly. "Actually, he just got out of surgery. Right now he's sitting in his office twiddling his thumbs. He asked me to come down for some fresh coffee and a pastry. He likes that afternoon sugar high. Does he know you're here?"

"Well . . . actually, no. I was . . . I was thinking of . . . surprising him. I'm caught up at the factory, so I thought . . ."

Alice winked like they were conspirators. "I can let him know you're here, Hannah, or you can go up. There aren't any more patients scheduled for today. He's been a bit of a bear lately, but I guess you know that. I'm thinking of cutting back on my own hours. I should have retired a year ago, but Dr. Kelly needed me back then. Now, he spends most of his time going over his cases with the team of doctors taking over his practice for when he leaves in January. But then you know all about that, too. We are certainly going to miss him and Dr. Wineberg when they go next year. I'm sure their patients are going to miss them just as much. They're both such excellent, caring doctors. I really need to get a move on. Dr. Kelly can get rambunctious when his orders aren't followed. It was nice to see you, Hannah."

Hannah watched as the nurse entered the coffee shop. For one intense moment, she thought she was going to black out. Her stomach started to roil, her head pounded, and her heart felt like it was going to leap right out of her chest. She had to pull herself together. She took great, gulping breaths in order to try and calm down. When Alice exited the coffee shop, Hannah stood up, pasting a sickly smile on her face. "Listen, Alice, don't tell Zack I'm here. I just had a brilliant idea, and I'm going to act on it. There are other ways to surprise one's husband. Promise?"

Alice winked. "Promise."

Hannah waited until the elevator closed behind the nurse before she bolted from the hospital lobby and out to her car. Inside, with the engine and heater running, she started to shake. She clamped her trembling hands over her ears as she tried to drown out the nurse's words that had so rocked her world. What did it all mean?

Zack and Joel were leaving in January! Why? Did Zack and Joel plan to sell their practices and not tell her and Sara? Where was he going in January? Hannah's stomach heaved when she realized January was just five and a half weeks away. When was he going to tell her? Was he *ever* going to tell her? Was this the first step in a plan to leave her? To divorce her? How could the world as she knew it fall apart so quickly? Was he going somewhere with another woman? Did he just plan on walking out on her with no explanation? She wondered who else knew about her husband's plans. Alice seemed to think she knew all about it.

A sound of pure agony escaped her lips. Somehow, some way, this had to be all her fault.

Tears rolled down Hannah's cheeks as she

slipped the car into gear. She drove aimlessly, through neighborhoods she didn't recognize. Should she go home? Or should she go back to the office? She needed to talk to someone. For the first time in her life she didn't want to share her misery with Sam or Sara. She should tell Sara, but she knew she'd never be able to get the words past her lips. *Why is that?* she wondered. Like Sam, she suddenly longed for a best friend.

Dad. Maybe she could talk to her father. A man's perspective. Then there was Ezra. What she should do, what she'd always done when something overwhelmed her, was go to Cisco. That probably wasn't a good idea. Cisco was consumed with business in the valley and getting ready to move into her new house. If she went to Cisco, Cisco would smother her with love, and she would comfort her, but there would be no answers. The answers would have to come from inside herself. *Damn, here I am worrying about answers, and I don't even know the question.*

Hannah was suddenly aware of the snow flurries hitting the windshield. It hadn't snowed in the valley in November for a long time, years actually. The next thing she realized she was on the secondary road that led to where the construction was going on. She drove slowly, her eyes searching for her father's car. *I should have brought coffee or something,* she thought, when she saw his car parked on the side of the road. She saw him then, a hard hat on his head and a stack of two-by-fours on his shoulder. She hopped out of the car and ran toward him. "Hey, Dad, you got a minute?"

Jonathan Cisco turned to look at his daughter. He smiled. "What brings you out here, Hanny? I have a minute, but let me get these two-by-fours to Henry. It's snowing, as you can see. Bad weather means we're going to continue working around the clock. Your grandmother wants everyone in their new houses by Thanksgiving. Wait for me in your car, where it's warm."

Hanny made her way back to the car and turned on the engine. She flicked the heater to seventy and waited. What was she going to say? How should she say it? Should she just blurt everything out? Maybe she shouldn't say anything. Was she so stupid she couldn't solve her own problems? Why did she need to talk everything to death? *Because it's always been like that,* she answered herself.

Minutes later, Jonathan opened the door and removed his hard hat. "You didn't tell me, what brings you out to the valley, baby? You look . . . worried. Did you lose weight, Hanny?"

Hanny threw herself at her father. Clumsily, he wrapped his arms around her. "What is it? Are you sick? Did something happen to Sam or Sara? Mom was out here earlier, so I know she's all right. What is it, Hanny? Come on, share," he cajoled.

Hannah moved back to her side of the car. "Do I look stupid to you, Dad?"

Jonathan threw back his head and laughed. "Not one little bit. What's this all about? Make it quick, I have to get back to work."

Hannah told him. "I don't know what to do, Dad."

Jonathan watched the swirling snow slapping against the windshield. "I don't see Zack or Joel as shallow men resorting to tawdry affairs. Their reputations could be permanently damaged. As to their respective practices, I don't know what to tell you. You have to talk to your husband, Hanny. There can't be secrets in a marriage. I told you that the day of your wedding. That was a promise your mother and I made to one another the day we got married. The other promise she insisted on was that we would never go to bed angry with each other. I can't make this right for you. All I can do is listen. Would you look at that snow! I hope it doesn't stick. I'm sorry, Hanny, the men are waiting for me. Perhaps you should talk to Sam and Sara." He reached for the door handle.

Hannah's hand snaked out. "Wait, Dad. I was hoping . . . I thought . . . maybe you could talk to Alice. You know, see what you can find out for me."

Jonathan whirled around. "You want me to do your dirty work, is that it, Hannah? You're talking to the wrong person. This is your problem. I will not sneak around and spy for you because you lack the courage to confront Zack yourself. I really think you underestimate your husband, and for that I am truly sorry. I'm sorry, but I have to go. The people over there," he said, pointing to the construction site, "are waiting for me. They're depending on me. I made a promise to see this through. We all know how important promises are, don't we, Hanny?"

Hannah watched her father walk through the squalling snow. "Well, I guess he told me," she muttered to herself. "And he told me with gusto!"

Hannah turned her car around and drove back the way she had come, her thoughts chaotic. She headed back to the office. Her father was so right. *And now what? I can sleep on the cot in the little efficiency apartment Cisco had built for late nights.* The bathroom had a shower that was used only by family members. It would be the ideal place for her to hang out until she figured out what to do. If she was careful, no one would ever know she was staying at the factory. Just the thought of going home knowing what she now knew made her cringe. Staying at Cisco Candies was the perfect solution for the moment.

A U-turn was called for, and Hannah made it. She drove home, packed a bag, and put it in the trunk of the car. As she drove back to Cisco Candies she couldn't ever remember being so unhappy. "Oh, God, Mom, I wish you were here," she whispered over and over.

Sam worked steadily until seven o'clock, when he shut off his computer, put on his coat, and closed his office door. The building was exceptionally quiet. Sara's office was dark. Only in Hannah's office did lights glow. He yelled, "Good night," and continued down the hall. If his sister answered him, he didn't hear her. He shrugged as he left the building, comfortable knowing that the nighttime security system would click into place automatically.

He was glad to see that the light snow that had fallen earlier had stopped. The wind was strong, though, pushing him toward his four-by-four. He wondered what the next day's weather was supposed to be.

Sam's thoughts were still on Sonia and the fact that he was going to become a father. The same thoughts that had been with him all day as he made his way home to shower and shave. He was actually looking forward to having dinner with his dad. He couldn't wait to tell him about Billy Rutherford and their weekend get-together. He shivered with cold, and anticipation.

His house was dark when he pulled into the driveway. He knew it would be, but it still bothered him. He really needed to think about getting a dog. The thought was so ridiculous, he snorted. If he couldn't hang on to a wife, what made him think he could hold on to a dog. The next morning, when he left for the office, he'd leave lights on to avoid coming home to a dark house. Somewhere inside, probably the garage, he had some timers he could set. It was a bogus solution to his problem, and he knew it.

There were no messages on his voice mail. Even the telemarketers were leaving him alone.

It took Sam twenty-five minutes to shower

and shave. He dressed in dark brown corduroys and a hunter green turtleneck Sonia had given him the previous Christmas. When he reached the front door for his down jacket, he yanked the scarf that was stuck in the sleeve and threw it on the window seat. It was a bright red muffler made by Hanny, with holes every inch or so. When he'd asked his sister what the holes were for, she'd yanked the scarf back and sewn big buttons over the holes. Hannah needed to find a different pastime.

Sum Sun, the town's most popular eatery, was centrally located. Sam loved it because of the privacy it afforded. Mr. Sum believed in green plants and partitions, along with oriental paintings and statues that guaranteed that privacy. You could be sitting right behind your neighbor and never know it. He and Sonia used to eat there at least once a week. He knew for a fact that Sara and Hanny ate there regularly. So did Cisco.

Mr. Sum's youngest daughter, Aiko, smiled at him. Sam noticed one of her textbooks open on the desk. "Your usual table, Mr. Sam? Will anyone be joining you this evening?"

"The usual table is fine. My father will be joining me."

"Would you like some tea, or would you

150

prefer a drink, Mr. Sam?"

"Tea's good, Aiko. How's school?"

"The social side or the academic side?" Aiko twinkled.

"Both."

"I am on an even keel. Everything is fine, Mr. Sam. I'm on the Dean's List this semester. Papa Sum is very proud of me."

Sam smiled. "And well he should be."

"Simi will bring your tea. Will your father wish tea also?"

"Yes. Tomorrow is a workday, so it's tea for us."

Sam leaned back in the bright red leather booth and looked around. He liked all things oriental. The silk tapestries on the wall intrigued him. The black lacquer furnishings were pleasing to the eye. Sonia said Sum Sun's was the cleanest restaurant she'd ever eaten in.

At this time of evening he knew the restaurant was full, but he was hard-pressed to see or hear the customers, thanks to Mr. Sum's wife's decorating skill.

Simi, another Sum daughter, set down a pot of tea and two cups. Duck sauce, hot mustard, and a bowl of hard noodles followed. She smiled, bowed, then backed away. A minute later, Aiko escorted his father to the booth.

"Enjoy your dinners."

"It's cold out there," Jonathan said, shrugging out of his jacket. "The clock over the bank said it's twenty-seven degrees. At least it's not snowing." He rubbed his cold hands together to make his point. "So, son, how's it going? Any problems today?"

"Nope. If two massive orders hadn't come in around noon, I would have finished your work and my own. Sara has been courting two potential accounts in Washington, DC. Today they came through. Big-time. Both are specialty stores, and they want product the day after Thanksgiving. Get this, Dad. One store wants a thousand gift baskets filled with the piña colada caramels. Appropriately wrapped. I turned it right over to Sara, who then turned it over to Hanny because she has the decorating and packaging end down pat. The other account, another specialty store in Crystal City outside of DC, wants basically the same thing; but they want red ribbons on the baskets, whereas the other wants gold trimmings. I guaranteed delivery even if I have to drive to DC myself. A lot of last-minute orders came in, but none as large as those two. It's not a problem, Dad. How's it going with all the building?"

"Just fine."

"You look tired, Dad."

"I am tired, son, but it's a good tired. I sleep like the proverbial log. You don't look tired, Sam, you look . . . miserable."

"I guess that's because I am miserable. I'm going to work this all out. I'm getting the shrimp lo mein, how about you?"

"The same for me. This tea is just right." Jonathan leaned back in the booth and brought his finger to his lips at the same time. He jerked his thumb to the other side of the mahogany railing lined with green plants. He mouthed the words, "Zack and Joel."

Sam's eyebrows shot upward. "I think we need to listen to this," Jonathan hissed. "Slide closer to the railing. I'll explain later, Sam."

Sam waited to do his father's bidding until Simi returned to take their order. Then he slid to the end of the booth and tilted his head. His father did the same thing. They listened unashamedly.

On the other side of the screen, the two doctors raised their beer glasses to one another. "Good day or bad day?" Joel asked. He reached for a handful of hard noodles and crunched down.

"Same old, same old. Actually, it was a boring day. How was your day?"

"Hectic. When you're dealing with kids it's always a hectic day. I lanced two boils, set a broken thumb, sewed up a dog bite, doctored twenty-seven colds and sinus infections. Had four ear infections. Three bad tonsil cases. The list is endless. Any word from Hannah today?"

"She didn't come home last night. I told you that on the phone this morning. So, to answer your question, no, there was no call today. I guess I did a good job of ticking her off last night."

"This is all wrong, Zack. C'mon, let's get back on track here. We have to tell our wives. Like real soon. Are we still on for dinner tomorrow with Marylee and Corinne?"

"I haven't heard anything to the contrary, so we're still on. I made the reservation for eight tomorrow at the Barb Wire. Personally speaking, I can't wait. Let's talk about something else. I'm having the hot-and-sour soup and spareribs."

Joel snapped open his menu even though he knew what he was going to order. He didn't know why, but he wanted the last word. "Okay, if things go as planned tomorrow night, then we tell our wives. Agreed?" Zack mumbled a response Jonathan and Sam couldn't hear. "It's not going to be pretty, Zack. We waited too long. In fact, I think it's safe to say it's going to get down-right ugly."

On the other side of the railing and greenery, Sam Cisco's eyes popped wide, but no wider than his father's. He moved and was half out of the booth when his father reached for his arm, forcing him back into his seat. "Not now, Sam. We need to think about this," Jonathan whispered.

CHAPTER EIGHT

It was nine-thirty when Joel parked his car in the driveway. He sat for a moment, his shoulders slumped, his body bone weary. He took a moment to stare at the frosty star-filled night through the windshield of his car. He forced himself to get out of the car. His stomach in knots, he shuffled forward.

As he entered the house through the kitchen door, Joel realized that there were no tantalizing aromas, no cozy place settings at the table. Of late, those memories were just that, memories. Sara making a statement, and he couldn't blame her. He could hear faint voices; the television was on in the family room. Sara would be curled up in the corner of the big brown sofa they'd picked out together. There would be a fire, and Sara would be sipping a glass of wine. Her leftover dinner, probably soup and a sandwich, or the remains of it, would be on a TV tray. Sara might even be asleep with an afghan made by Hannah covering her.

He hung up his coat, dropped his medical bag on the counter, and walked into the family room. It was a wonderful room, designed for a large family. He loved the fieldstone fireplace and the floor-to-ceiling bookshelves. It was cozy and warm, like Sara herself. His wife was right where he knew she would be. The fire was blazing, the red-and-white afghan wrapped around her. Her dinner — soup and a sandwich — were on a tray at the end of the couch, untouched; her wineglass was still full.

"Hi, Sara." *Now that was brilliant.*

Sara looked up, smiled, and waved. "Darn it! I must have missed the announcement that the world was coming to an end. You're home before midnight."

It wasn't said sarcastically, it was said with sadness. A lump formed in Joel's throat as he approached the sofa. He dropped to his haunches in front of Sara and reached for her hands. "Look at me, Sara. I want to tell you something, and I also want to ask you something. Keep looking at me, honey. Don't look away. I want you to know I love you with all my heart. I want you to know my life wasn't complete until I met you. I know I've been all doctor lately and very little husband. I'm going to change that. I don't know how, but I am. Now, for my question. Keep looking at me, Sara. Do you love me as much as I love you?"

Tears glistened in Sara's eyes. "Yes, Joel, I do love you. More than I can ever tell you. Maybe I haven't been a good wife either. I truly, truly understand about your patients. Children . . . the children need you, but I need you, too. I know that sounds selfish, but I need you. We have to figure something out because I don't want to live alone, and I *am* living alone, Joel."

"I know. Can I sit there next to you?"

Sara reached for his tie and yanked him forward. He kissed her then with such passion, Sara turned weak. "Wow!"

Joel took a deep breath. "Yeah, wow. The *wow* has to come later, Sara. I need to talk to you about something important. I want you to hear me out and not say anything until I finish. Then we're going to talk, and after that we're going to go for the WOW part, okay?"

Sara scrunched into him and pulled Joel's face close to her own. "Something's wrong. What? What is it, Joel? Tell me. Is this where you tell me you're having an affair and you're leaving me? Who is she, Joel?"

Joel's eyes literally bugged out of his head.

His whole body grew hot with shame and guilt. "What? What are you talking about? Why would you think I'm having an affair? Where did you get such an idea?"

Sara drew back, her eyes cold and hard. "I asked you a question. I expect an answer. Instead, you're asking me more questions. If you think for one minute I'm falling for that *WOW* thing, you're all wrong. Good night, Dr. Wineberg. You can sleep in the guest room tonight and every other night from here on."

Joel watched as his wife stomped out of the room, her back stiff as a board, her head high. He should run after her, explain about the boat, but he'd promised Zack he'd wait. It was such a stupid promise, but he'd made it, and he would live with it for one more day.

One more day!

An affair! Where did Sara get such an idea? How could she even think such a thing? He'd just declared his love for her, and she'd declared hers in return. And now this. "I'm going to strangle you, Zack!" he muttered as he stretched out on the sofa. He didn't have the energy to climb the steps to the guest room. He didn't have the energy for *anything*.

Sam sat in his truck in the parking lot of Biffy's Breakfast Bar chomping on a bacon-and-egg sandwich, his mind whirling and twirling. He hadn't even bothered to go to sleep when he returned to the house after dinner with his father. All he could think about was his wife, her pregnancy, and the possibility that he would have to go to the other side of the world to see his child when it was born. When he couldn't stand thinking about his wife and unborn child anymore, he thought about Zack Kelly and his sister Hanny, and Joel and Sara. He shivered inside his down jacket even though the truck heater was running full blast. For the moment there was little he could do about Sonia, but he could do something about Zack if he wanted to. *If* he wanted to. Just the thought of punching the doctor out was so pleasing, he grew dizzy. If there was one thing in this world he hated, it was a cheating spouse.

He finished his sandwich, gulped at the scalding coffee, barely noticing how hot it was. He was damn sick and tired of secrets, promises, and tiptoeing through the tulips where everyone was concerned.

Sam slumped farther back into the seat, his head resting on the leather headrest. He closed his eyes. If he couldn't salvage his own life, maybe he could help Hanny and Sara. He clenched his teeth in frustration at all the things he'd overheard Joel and Zack discuss. Then he thought about his father's warning not to stick his nose where it didn't belong. Good advice. Well, someone had to do something.

Sam bolted upright, slammed the Rover into reverse, and barreled out of the parking lot. It was still dark, and there was little traffic on the secondary roads, but it would be light soon, and rush-hour traffic, such as it was, would start up.

He was relieved to see Zack's car in the driveway and lights on in the house. Zack hadn't left yet. Time to stick his nose into his brother-in-law's business. If his nose got smacked, so be it.

Zack was in the kitchen eating a banana and drinking coffee. He was dressed for the day in a blue suit, pristine white shirt, and red-striped tie. Zack had two modes of dress, fashion plate or beach bum.

Sam rapped sharply on the door. His brother-in-law looked up, his face registering surprise. He got up to open the door, his eyes full of questions he was afraid to ask. A family problem? Hannah? Sam never visited at this hour of the morning.

Sam walked over to the coffeepot, poured himself a cup of coffee he didn't want, turned around, and said, "I came here to talk, so sit down, Zack. If you don't sit down, or if you give me any crap, I'm going to punch your lights out. Now, sit!" He glared at Zack to make his point.

Zack sat. "What the hell's wrong with you, Sam?"

"You're what's wrong with me. Hannah is what's wrong with me. Sara's what's wrong with me. Joel's what's wrong with me. My father's what's wrong with me. Sonia, who by the way left me because she's pregnant, and didn't bother to tell me, is what's wrong with me, and Cisco is what's wrong with me.

"For starters, I'm damn sick and tired of secrets and promises. Did anyone ever tell you Cisco used to dress the three of us alike? We were like three little monkeys performing on the stage of life? Our mother always dressed us differently. She treated us as individuals. Dad went with the flow. He never wanted to go into the candy business, but he had three kids to support. He always wanted to work with his hands, to build furniture and maybe someday houses.

Pretty damn sad, huh? Don't interrupt, I have a lot more to say.

"Did you ever notice that Sara, Hannah, and I have no friends? We don't. We three were an island unto ourselves. That's pretty damn sad, too. But, that's going to change. Do you have any cigarettes?"

Zack looked dazed. "Cigarettes? I didn't know you smoked. No, I don't have any cigarettes. I have some cigars, though. Sam, what's this all about?"

"I don't smoke. But I'll take a cigar."

Confused and bewildered, Zack opened the cabinet and took two cigars out of a box.

"We probably should have some brandy in this coffee if we're going to smoke these cigars. You got any?" Sam snarled. "You aren't very hospitable, Zack."

Still confused and bewildered, Zack got up again and brought out a brandy bottle. He poured liberally into both cups. He sat back down and waited.

The kitchen slowly filled with cigar smoke. Both men ignored it.

Sam paced the kitchen as Zack eyed him warily.

Sam's eyes narrowed. "Do you love my sister?" Zack's head bobbed up and down.

Sam moved then like a stalking panther as he grabbed Zack's tie and literally lifted him out of his chair before letting him down. He was in his brother-in-law's face a second later. "Oh, yeah, then how come you haven't told her about Marylee and Corinne? My father and I heard you and Joel last night at Sum Sun's. We were sitting on the other side of the railing."

Zack licked his lips. "That's another dumb-ass question, Sam." He reached for the bottle and took a hearty gulp. Sam did the same thing.

"Answer me, or I'll beat the hell out of you," Sam threatened.

Zack looked up at his brother-in-law, trying to decide if Sam meant what he said or not. He yanked at his tie and pulled it over his head. He pitched it over his shoulder. "Because."

Sam blew a puff of cigar smoke in Zack's direction. "My sister loves you. I'm not going to let you break her heart just because you're stupid."

Zack reared up in his chair. "I'm a doctor. That means I'm smart. Don't call me dumb again. You don't look real smart to me right now either. You just admitted you didn't know your wife is pregnant. How smart is *that?* It's not what you think, and, besides, it's none of your damn business. You don't see me sticking my nose into your life, do you? That's because I respect you. Now, take your smelly cigar and brandy and get the hell out of my house. *NOW!*"

"I'll go when I'm damn good and ready to go and not one minute sooner," Sam snarled.

Zack's jacket sailed over his shoulder and landed on top of the red-striped tie. He knew he wasn't going to the office today. He eyed the brandy bottle at Sam's lips. Sam wasn't going to the factory either. He grinned at his assessment. That had to mean he was smart. Sam was full of hot air.

"Are you going to tell Hannah what you heard, Sam?"

"No. That's *your* place, but if you *don't* tell her, I will. Make some more coffee, Zack."

"Why should I?" Zack asked, his voice laced with belligerence. He wondered if he was drunk.

"Because I'm the guy's who's going to knock your block off if you don't. Tell Hannah you made a mistake. Everyone makes mistakes. I'm warning you, if you don't tell her, I will. Enough is enough now. You're both a pair of jerks in my opinion."

"You know, Sam, I don't appreciate you sticking your nose into my business. I didn't ask for your help. I can handle this by myself. My point being you don't have a clue as to what Joel and I were really discussing. I'd like you to leave now before we say things to each other we'll both regret. I'll take care of my wife in my own way without any help from you."

Sam sat down and watched the coffee drip into the pot. It was like he hadn't heard a word Zack said. "Do you have any idea how much I envy your relationship with Joel? You are one lucky son of a gun to have a friend who cares about you as much as Joel cares about you.

"Sara, Hannah, and I never had real, true friends. All of our lives are messed up right now. I can't quite put my finger on what brought it all to a head at this point in time. It was going downhill even before the tornado wiped out Cisco's house. There was one wild, crazy instant when I was glad it happened. That probably doesn't make sense to you. Hell, it doesn't make sense to me. The best I can come up with is I saw it as a new beginning, a way to leave the ghosts of the past behind. Then again, maybe it was Hannah and you that brought everything to a head. Or it could be Sonia walking out on me. It's my goal in life to make us as whole as we can be. In order to do that, we all have to pull together. I'm sick and tired of being isolated with only my sisters for friends. I want to find my wife and mend my own bridges. I might need your help, Joel's, too. I want to know if I can count on you. I guess what I'm trying to say is, we all need each other. I came here to offer my help if you need it."

Zack tilted his chair backward, his gaze steady and unblinking. "Let's deal with you first. You want to talk about this, Sam? I'm a good listener. No promises. Like you, I'm sick of secrets and promises." He stood up and walked toward his brother-in-law.

Sam stared at Zack for several minutes. All he could see was hope and compassion, even relief, in Zack's expression. Satisfied with what he was seeing, Sam's hand shot out. Zack grasped it as he hooked his foot under the rung of the wooden chair to bring it closer. He sat down, his eyes steady and alert. Sam did the same thing.

"Okay, let's talk."

"I want to talk about my mom, then I want to talk about you," Sam said.

"I'm listening, Sam."

It was noon when Zack walked to the door with Sam. They did the guy thing, clapping each other on the back, then shaking hands. When the door closed behind Sam, Zack walked back toward the kitchen. For a moment he felt like he could conquer the world. The last time he'd felt this good was the day he'd made the decision to buy the boat, his lifelong dream. He couldn't help but wonder if the good feeling had anything to do with the brandy he and Sam had consumed. "Nah," he mumbled as he set about cleaning up the kitchen.

The phone rang as he stacked the cups in the dishwasher. He didn't feel like answering it, but he was a doctor. He listened to his nurse Alice as she inquired about his well-being.

"No, Alice, I'm not coming in today. Ask Jonesy," he said, referring to a fellow physician, "if he'll do me a favor and check Mr. Rosen for me. Tell him I owe him one. What am I doing? I'm doing the dishes, then I'm going for a run. What do you mean why do I sound so chipper? I always sound chipper. I am not an ogre, and you know it. Hey, I might not be in tomorrow either. You okay with that, Alice? Good. Stay in touch. Refer any emergencies to Jonesy. I'll call him later. Stop fussing, Alice, I'm fine."

And he was fine.

Zack made his way upstairs, where he changed his clothes. The fleece-lined warm-up suit felt good. There was no doubt in his mind that he could do the full ten miles. Thanks to Sam. He headed for the door, then turned back to sit down on the king-size bed. Everything in the room smelled like Hannah. Everything.

Damn, how could I have been so blind? How could I not have seen what she was going through?

"Oh, God, Hanny, did I drive you away from me the other night? How in the hell am I going to make that right? Sam said, you just do it, that's how. You go to her like the stupid jerk you are, and you tell her the way it is. Remind her that she's a stupid jerk herself sometimes. End of story." Ever-blunt Sam.

It sounded like a plan. Sam said pride was a deadly sin. Sam had an answer for everything. When had Sam gotten so smart?

Well, he was going to have to think about this. It couldn't be as simple and as easy as Sam made it sound.

Zack reached for his Walkman and clamped the earphones on his head. He'd think about his problem on his run. Then when he got home, he'd build a fire, pop something in the oven, and sit and work out the best way to approach his wife tonight after his and Joel's dinner with their instructors, Marylee and Corinne.

CHAPTER NINE

Loretta Cisco walked through her new little house in the valley. A fire burned in the new fireplace. A brand-new blanket and two new dog beds sat beside the hearth waiting for Freddie and Hugo to accept them. So far the dogs had just sniffed at them. Freddie looked up at her mistress. Cisco leaned down, and whispered, "Like Sam says, Freddie, it sucks, but we have to accept it. I don't like all this new stuff either." She stroked the retriever's golden head with a gnarled hand. The dog inched her toward the new recliner that sat in the same place the old one had rested.

Cisco sat down, her face puckering, as she tried not to cry. Freddie dropped her head in her lap and licked her hand.

"Frederica," Cisco said to the dog, "in fifty years it will be like our old house. We just have to make this new house lived in. Maybe when we get some Christmas decorations up it will look different. Would you listen to me? Tomorrow is Thanksgiving, and here I am thinking about Christmas."

Cisco looked up to see Ezra standing in the doorway. "It smells so new," she observed. Fresh paint, wallpaper in the bathrooms, and the new wood smell, not to mention the furniture polish. I guess we should go to a flower shop to get some green plants. Green plants always seem to make a house look more lived in. The fire is nice, Ezra, thank you for building it."

Ezra marched around the cozy living room looking at the different pieces of new furniture, touching a table, smoothing the arm covers on the sofa. "Before you know it, Loretta, you'll have this house filled with new memories and new treasures. Right now it looks a tad bare because there are no pictures on the walls, and like you said, green plants will make a big difference.

"I have an idea, Loretta. Do you remember the pictures we took on Labor Day? The film is still in my camera up at my house. Let's take them to be developed, then frame them so you have pictures on your mantel. We need to buy the dogs some new toys, too. If we leave now, we'll be back in plenty of time for you to make the pies for Thanksgiving dinner at the church tomorrow. I promised I would help, and I will."

Cisco heaved herself out of the new recliner. "It's fairly comfortable. Did you try yours out yet, Ezra?"

"No, but I will later when the pies are baking," Ezra said, laughing.

"Tell me again why we aren't having Thanksgiving dinner here in my new house."

"We are not having dinner here because Jonathan and the Trips have other things to do. Let's not dwell on that, Loretta. Father Drupieski convinced us the town needs to come together for Thanksgiving dinner at the church. If I'm not mistaken, it was your idea, Loretta. You can't wiggle out now. Everyone is bringing something, like you suggested. Father himself is roasting the turkeys. We have so much to be thankful for, my dear."

Cisco squared her shoulders. Everything Ezra said was true. Why was she having so much trouble accepting things as they were now? In addition, she was thinking way too much, and she wasn't liking the direction her thoughts were taking. "You're saying I prefer living in the past with my memories. That's partly true, but this will be the first year ever that I didn't make Thanksgiving dinner for my family. My biggest fear, my

172

only fear, is that the family will be too busy this Christmas to come home. What will I do then? How will I handle that, Ezra?"

"I don't know, Loretta. I just know you will. We are getting married Christmas Day, so that will be a new beginning for both of us. I think that's what we have to concentrate on, not on what might or might not happen."

Cisco managed a wan smile. "When all is said and done, Ezra, it always comes down to family. We've come so far, been through so much, I don't want to see it all disappear. There's trouble with my Trips. There's trouble with Jonathan. In the past they always confided in me. But not this time. That's how I know this time is serious and different."

"Do you think it has something to do with me?" Ezra asked hesitantly.

"Oh, good Lord, no, Ezra. My family loves you as much as I do. No, it's something else they've chosen not to share with me. The not sharing is the part that bothers me. I'm having a real hard time with it."

"The Trips are married now, Cisco. That changes everything. They share with their husbands, and that's as it should be. In addition, you turned over the business to them. I'm afraid it's something we're going to have to get used to. It was bound to be painful, Loretta. We talked about this if you recall."

They were in the new kitchen by then. Cisco looked down at the electric range, with its smooth glass top. She moved on to the built-in dishwasher and the monster refrigerator. Everything matched and sparkled. Even the trash compactor. "New-fangled appliances. I bet that stove doesn't bake half as good as my old one." She looked up at the kitchen window. It cried for a green plant and a set of cheerful curtains. "But it's so out of character for the Trips. They don't even call anymore, Ezra."

"Yes, Loretta, they do call. They just don't stay on the line and jabber endlessly. They also leave messages when we aren't home now that I got an answering machine. In addition, you don't care for the things they say. I think, my dear, if you had your way, you'd keep them as children all their lives."

Cisco pursed her lips. Sometimes Ezra was too smart for his own good. She walked over to the new rocking chair, with its new checkered cushions, in front of the kitchen fireplace, and sat down. She motioned for Ezra to sit on the companion rocker. "The rock is off. I'll get used to it," she added hastily as she saw the look of exasperation on Ezra's face. "I used to dress the Trips alike when they were young. Right after Margie died. It seemed important to do that. To make them one, if that makes any sense. Sam rebelled, but his father stepped in, and that was the end of that. He wanted to wear jeans with holes in the knees, dirty sneakers, and ragged shirts. Margie let him dress like that. She was a wonderful wife and mother but extremely indulgent. Then when they went to private school, they had to wear uniforms that were alike. Sam rebelled at that, too. Somewhere along the way, he just gave in. They were so happy back then. We were all so happy.

"The children know every stone and blade of grass in this valley. The mountain, too. They played from morning till night in the summers. After chores of course. It was the happiest time of my life." Cisco sighed.

Ezra's brow furrowed. "It must have been hectic with their friends here all the time."

Cisco looked at him sharply before she rose out of the chair. "No, it wasn't hectic because there were no friends. The Trips didn't need friends; they had each other. Jonathan and I had the factory to run, and there was no time to arrange play dates. I think that's the term parents use today.

Trust me when I tell you they were extremely busy with piano lessons, dance lessons, gymnastics. We had instructors come out to the valley."

"Oh," was all Ezra could think of to say.

"Didn't you say you wanted to go to town? Let's go, Ezra. Strolling down Memory Lane is depressing. I think after the holidays I am going to get someone to wallpaper this kitchen. A white paper with clusters of strawberries all over it. Something cheerful. Maybe I'll get some red crockery. I have to get a new cookie jar, too, for Freddie's dog treats. A big red strawberry. I saw one in a catalog. I'm thinking I'm going to be shopping a lot through catalogs after Christmas. You know, when the snow starts to fall."

Ezra nodded. He wondered why Loretta's voice sounded so defensive. He shrugged. He was always careful not to step over the line Cisco had drawn earlier in regard to her precious Trips. Maybe that would change when they got married, and he became an official family member. Then again, maybe it wouldn't.

Cisco turned to lock the door behind them. This was new, too. She'd never, ever, locked her doors before. She wondered why she was doing it. She looked around, then

176

up at the sky. It was gray and dismal-looking, and it felt like snow was in the air. Already, her old bones were aching. She shivered as she made her way down the path that led to the driveway where Ezra's new truck waited, the engine running.

The holly bushes were full of succulent red berries, the spreading yews sparkling with icy crystals. Winter had definitely arrived. She shivered again inside her new coat. "When do you think Sam and Sonia are going to tell us about their pregnancy, Ezra?"

Ezra stopped in midstride. He turned to look at the little lady he'd come to love with such passion. "And you know this . . . how, Loretta?"

"Just by looking at Sonia. I noticed it a month ago when I saw Sonia. She has that look. Don't worry, Ezra, it's a woman thing. There's a certain sparkle in a woman's eyes when she's pregnant."

Ezra settled his baseball cap more firmly on his head. "I see. Is that what's been bothering you, Loretta? Careful now, step up on the running board. I had it installed just for you, you know. I can give you a *boost* if you need it," he joked.

"I do not need a boost, thank you very much. Yes, their not telling me that she's expecting bothers me, among other things. They should be shouting the news from the rooftops. When Margie got pregnant, everyone in the valley knew within an hour of her finding out. I don't think there was a happier woman on this earth that day. Oh, it's so warm," Cisco said as she slipped her seat belt into place.

"It's that newfangled gizmo that allows you to turn your engine on as well as the heater from inside the house. I got it just for you because I know how you hate to shiver, Loretta. You see, new things aren't so bad. Eventually you get used to them, then wonder how you ever did without them before."

"Hmmm. Let's take the long way into town, go around to the other side of the valley, Ezra, I want to see how Jonathan is doing with the Ryans' house. Ruth is expecting to move in today. She might need some help."

"By the long way, do you mean past the fifty acres of land you own on the other side of the valley?"

"Yes, dear, that way," Cisco replied absently as she stared out the window. "I really think it might snow before the day is over."

"Do you mind telling me why you want to go so far out of our way, Loretta? It's not that I mind, I just like to know the why of things. I think you might be right about the snow, too."

"Because."

Ezra concentrated on his driving. "Because" meant he wasn't going to get any further information. He glared at the road and tried not to think about his unhappy driving companion.

Hannah didn't hesitate when she parked her car in the lot of the Allegheny Inn. She hopped out, snapped the trunk open, and yanked out her bag. She walked forward quickly before she could change her mind. The move to the Inn was a necessity. She couldn't take one more night of sleeping on that uncomfortable cot at the factory. She probably wouldn't sleep here either, but at least she'd be in a comfortable bed and could watch television all night long.

She registered, accepted the key, and left her bag at the desk to be brought up later. For some reason she thought the Inn would be bustling with out-of-town visitors home for the holiday, but the lobby was almost empty. A few businessmen checking out, a few people she didn't recognize, and that was it. While she waited for the elevator, she looked around. Her parents' wedding reception had been held here at the Inn. It looked the same to her now as it had in the old pictures in Cisco's album. The album that was now gone, never to be replaced. The thought brought tears to her eyes.

The elevator swished open, and she came face-to-face with Sonia.

"Sonia!"

"Hannah!"

Both young women started to jabber at once, then stopped to stare at each other in confusion. It was Hannah who had the presence of mind to take hold of her sister-in-law's hand and draw her toward the huge fieldstone fireplace that took up one whole wall of the lobby. "Sam's been looking for you!" Hannah hissed. She yanked at two of the chairs and turned them so they faced the fire. She sat down and turned toward Sonia.

"You know, one year, someone chopped down a big old cherry tree in their yard and sawed the trunk into two parts, and brought it here to the Inn for this very fireplace. It took all of November and December for the first part to burn all the way through. It burned day and night. The second half burned through January and February. Imagine that! I read about it in the *Daily News.*

"We can order breakfast here. Cisco used to bring us here for Sunday brunch when we were little but only after we'd learned some manners. She spiffed us up to look like . . . oh, I don't know. Sam said we looked like the Three Stooges. People always stared at us. It got so I hated coming here. I don't think Sara liked it either. Talk to me, Sonia," Hannah said breathlessly.

Sonia was petite, with dark eyes and dark hair, and a winsome, endearing smile. *It's easy to see why Sam fell in love with her,* Hannah thought. "Listen, Sonia, I don't for one minute buy that story of you leaving Sam because you want bright lights and excitement. Now, tell me, what's going on between you and Sam? Why did you leave him? He's devastated. On top of being devastated, he's someone I don't even know anymore. It's not just because you left him, Sonia. It's something else. All of a sudden it's like he and Sara and I are all unraveling. We thought you went home to your parents." This was also said breathlessly. She tugged at the hunter green jacket of her pantsuit, which felt too big.

"I didn't have enough money to go to my parents," Sonia explained. "As a matter of fact, I can only stay here one more day, then I was going to . . . I don't know what I was going to do. Go to Father Drupieski and ask for help I guess. What are you doing here, Hannah?"

Hannah leaned back in the chair and rattled off her story. It was such a relief to talk about it to someone other than her family, not that she didn't consider Sonia family. She was *new* family. When Hannah finally wound down, she said, "I'm just as displaced as you are. You can bunk with me here at the Inn until both of us decide what to do.

"Why did you run like that, Sonia? Why didn't you come to Sara or me?"

"I did tell Sara I was pregnant and swore her to secrecy. I didn't want to cause problems between Sam and the two of you. It seemed like the best thing to do at the time, just as you thought it was best to hide your fear that your husband is having an affair, which, by the way, I don't believe."

Sonia sighed. "I don't know how it happened, Hannah. Sam and I used birth control, and still I got pregnant. I knew he would blame me because I wanted children right away, and he didn't. We agreed to wait a year or two to have children. I was okay with that even though I wanted children right away. I understood. What I never understood was why Sam didn't want me to work. My parents sacrificed a lot to send me here to the States to go to college. I wanted to teach, and Sam wanted me to stay home. All I did was clean house and cook. It was what your mother did, and that's what he wanted me to do. Every time I brought up the subject of getting a job he'd get upset. I hate soap operas. I hate watching game shows. I got tired of scrubbing and cleaning. I was so desperate to do something, I started mowing the lawn so Sam wouldn't have to do it. I planted flowers, painted the back porch. I even black-topped the driveway. He was furious. And then I got pregnant. Do you think you could lend me money to go home, Hannah?"

"Of course I can lend you money to go home, but that isn't your answer, Sonia. Your answer is to talk to Sam. Work it out. At least try. If that doesn't work, then you can go home. I think you might have finally gotten Sam's attention. He loves you with all his heart, Sonia. He really does."

Sonia's smile stretched from ear to ear. "You know this for sure, Hannah?"

Hannah smiled in return. "I know this for sure. Let's get some breakfast. The coffee shop here at the Inn makes a wonderful omelet." Realizing Sonia's finances were on the low side, she said, "I insist, and it's my treat."

"This is a very pleasant lobby. I've been coming down in the evenings to sit by the fire and read the paper. I met some lovely people. Two of them actually invited me for Thanksgiving dinner. Of course I said no. Are you going to your grandmother's, Hannah?"

"No. I'm probably going to eat right here at the hotel, or else I'll go over to the church. The whole town will turn out for Thanksgiving dinner. Maybe we should think about going together. You know, strength in numbers, that kind of thing. Call me stubborn or whatever you want, but I'm not going home to a cold house and a husband who doesn't want me and is unfaithful in the bargain. I'm too worn-out emotionally to fight with Zack. I'm willing to take the blame for my end of things, but I'm not taking the blame for everything. I have my pride, too. I'm sick and tired of being alone. At least you can't say that about Sam. Sara and I have spent so much time alone we could be classified as widows. Look, let's talk about pleasant things."

Hannah and Sonia gave their orders to a perky young woman with freckles and red ribbons in her hair. A coffeepot was placed in front of them. Hannah was pouring coffee into their cups when she sensed a presence behind her. She turned and looked up, a questioning expression on her face.

"Excuse me, but aren't you one of the Cisco triplets? I'm taking a wild guess here, but I'd say you're Hannah." The man's hand shot out. "I'm Bill Rutherford. Sam and I used to be best buddies. This lovely, very pregnant creature next to me is my wife, Julie. We came back for Thanksgiving dinner at the church. Father Drupieski and your father invited us."

"Billy! My gosh. You grew up," Hannah said inanely. "This is my sister-in-law, Sonia," Hannah said brightly. Let him draw his own conclusions, she thought.

Bill laughed. "So did you."

An awkward silence followed. "Would you like to join us?" The instant the words were out of Hannah's mouth she regretted them. Sonia looked like a deer caught in the headlights.

"Sure, if you don't mind."

Chairs shuffled, more silverware and napkins and coffee cups were added to the table. The Rutherfords ordered ham-and-mushroom omelets, the same thing Sonia and Hannah had ordered.

Hannah crossed her fingers under the

table that Bill wouldn't ask what they were doing at the Inn. She grappled in her mind for a safe topic of conversation. Childhood should be a safe topic she thought. She plunged ahead. "Gee, when was the last time we saw one another?"

"A hundred years ago." Bill laughed.

Hannah sensed he didn't want to go down Memory Lane any more than she did.

"Imagine my surprise when Sam called me a few days ago. It was like old times all over again. He was going to travel up to Johnstown this weekend to see me, but I think we both forgot it was Thanksgiving weekend. I'm looking forward to seeing him tomorrow and spending time with him."

"How nice for both of you," Hannah said.

"We're moving back to the valley next summer. Julie and I want to raise our kids here. Your dad is going to build our house for us as soon as we find a lot. What do you think of *that?*"

Hannah didn't know what to think of *that.* She stared across the table at the man who had once been Sam's best friend. She felt a stab of nostalgia as a long-buried memory attacked her like a wild animal. It was a week or so after their mother's funeral, and Sam hadn't come into the house when Cisco called. It was dark when their father finally marched a belligerent Sam up the steps to his room, where he'd forced him to take off his tattered jeans and stretched-out T-shirt. Then he'd whipped Sam's butt. Not so much because he'd gone out to the main road that would take him to Billy Rutherford's house, but because he'd taken off his plaid shorts and red T-shirt and donned his old clothes. What Sam called his happy clothes. Sam hadn't cried or whimpered either. Nobody, least of all Sam, ever mentioned Billy Rutherford's name again.

Hannah knew she was supposed to say something because everyone was looking at her. "I didn't know Dad was going into the construction business." She wondered if she looked as stupid as she felt. Obviously Bill did because he just stared at her.

"Jeez, don't tell me I gave away some sort of secret here?"

Bill looked so agitated, Hannah took pity on him. She smiled. "That's just like Dad. He told me a day or so ago that he was thinking about it. I guess he made his decision. Lucky you."

"I'd say so. The valley is really growing. New businesses moving in every day, and the population has tripled in the last fifteen years. It might be rough going for a little while, but we'll manage, won't we, honey?"

Julie nodded, beaming with happiness.

Hannah listened as Bill droned on and on about the advantages of growing up in the valley and raising kids here. When he finally said, "I hate to eat and run, but Julie and I promised Father Drupieski we'd help him set up the tables at the church. I hope we get to see you there tomorrow." He reached for the check. Hannah was too tired to protest. She smiled as she shook hands.

When she was sure the Rutherfords were out of earshot she turned to Sonia. "I'm sorry, Sonia. He blindsided me. There was nothing else I could do."

"It's all right, Hannah. Sam used to talk about Billy Rutherford. He loved him like a brother. Did you know he always wanted a brother?"

"No, but that doesn't surprise me. He was surrounded by females all the time. Would you like to take a walk, Sonia? We need to talk. I find for some reason that I can think best when I'm out in the fresh air. Suddenly I don't think it's such a good idea for you to continue to stay here. After the walk, I'd like to drive you back to your house. You need to talk to Sam and settle your lives. If you can't come to terms, then I want you to come to me, and I'll get you a plane ticket home. On the other hand," she dithered, "we could both spend one more night here, go to the Thanksgiving dinner at the church, meet up with our husbands, *then* go back to our respective houses. See, how confused I get? That's why we need to walk and talk."

Sonia slipped into a bright red coat with a faux fur collar. She pulled on a pair of matching mittens made by Hannah. One of the thumbs was lopsided. "Yes, let's walk and talk. I don't know what I was trying to prove and to whom I was trying to prove it. I'm so glad you showed up when you did. I was literally at my wit's end. We should talk about you, Hannah. What can I do to help you?"

Hannah stared down at the petite young woman. The word *friend* came to mind.

Outside, the two women linked arms as they strode through the parking lot of the Inn.

New friends.

CHAPTER TEN

Hannah's cell phone rang shortly before seven-thirty that evening. Her greeting was cautious.

"Hanny, it's Sara. I'm just getting ready to leave work. I was wondering if you'd like to go out for a bite to eat. Plus, I don't really feel like going home. My treat, what do you say?"

Relieved to hear the sound of her sister's voice, Hannah said, "Sure. Listen, do you mind if Sonia comes along. I found her. She's staying here at the Inn. I literally bumped into her in the elevator. We pretty much spent the day together. She's as miserable as we are."

"That's great, Hanny. Of course you can bring her along. Where would you like me to meet you two?"

"I'm not in the mood for Chinese. That leaves us with Rafferty's, the Pickle Barrel, or the Barb Wire."

"Rafferty's is usually too crowded, and you can't hear yourself think. I'm not into deli food, so that leaves us the Barb Wire. I'll meet you there in thirty minutes."

"See you there then, sis. Hey, you okay?"

"I'm about as good as you are, Hanny. Is Sonia okay?"

"She's in the same emotional state we're in. Health-wise, she's fine. See you in half an hour."

Hannah turned to Sonia, and said. "Let's freshen up, we're going out to dinner with Sara. And guess what, Sassy Sara, a.k.a. Frugal Sara, is springing for the tab. We can't refuse."

Sonia smiled wanly as she followed Hannah to the elevator.

"I'll meet you down here in fifteen minutes. Put some lipstick on, Sonia, and some perfume. It will make you feel better. I'm going to do the same thing."

Thirty-five minutes later, Hannah rolled into the parking lot of the Barb Wire right behind her sister Sara. They parked side by side at the far end of the lot so they could exit the side street when it was time to leave, thereby avoiding the eighteen-wheelers that careened down the highway at high rates of speed day and night. Sara climbed out of the car at the same time Hannah and Sonia did. There were hugs and kisses, and good wishes for the expectant mother. "Isn't it amazing how we always manage to get the exact same parking spot?" Sara said.

"Yeah, it's downright amazing," Hannah mumbled. "I think it's starting to snow. Just what we need. Snow for Thanksgiving," she mumbled again.

Suddenly both Sara and Hannah felt a viselike grip on their arms. "Look," Sonia cried.

"Oh, no," Sara said brokenly.

"I'll kill him! I'll kill both of them," Hannah said, as Sonia pulled her and Sara farther away from the light between two parked cars where they were standing.

The three women watched as Zack and Joel escorted two striking-looking women toward the front door. The women were carrying what looked like gift-wrapped boxes. The foursome appeared to be in high spirits, as both doctors wrapped their arms around the women's shoulders.

"The blonde has legs that go up to her throat," Sara said in a choked voice.

"That suit has to be Escada. How can that redhead walk in those spike-heeled shoes?" Hannah asked brokenly.

"They look like models," Sonia said. She instantly regretted the words. "Come," she said, "we need to get in the car and talk about this." Sara and Hannah followed her blindly.

"I hate men," Sara said, the minute the car door closed behind her. "Just last night Joel said he loved me. See, see, you can never trust a man! You can trust Sam, Sonia," she added hastily. "What are we going to do, Hannah?"

"Killing them is too good. I say we go in there and confront them! I want to see the look on their faces when they see us. We'll wing the rest of it. How dare they humiliate us in public this way! Everyone inside that restaurant will be at the Thanksgiving dinner at the church tomorrow. They'll look at us with pity. Think how we're going to feel. I can't believe this! I knew it! I knew those two were up to something. Oh, God, Sara, did you see how beautiful those women are?"

"We look like Girl Scout leaders compared to them," Sara said, sniffling into a tissue. "Did you see those chic hairdos?" She ran her hand through her own short curly mop of hair to make her point. "Joel used to say my hair reminded him of Little Orphan Annie. Okay, what are we going to do?"

Hannah squared her shoulders. "For starters, we have to forget that those two weasels broke our hearts. Second, we need to get mad. *Really* mad. Then we're going to go in there and confront the aforesaid weasels. And, I don't think it's carved in stone that we have to act like ladies. Now, let's talk this through. Angie Loyd is the hostess. We both know her, so she won't try to stop us if we accost our husbands. Oh, that word sticks in my throat.

"Because men really know nothing about women, and for the most part they're dumber than women, I think it's safe to say when they made the dinner reservation, they asked for *our* favorite table. What that means is we know exactly where we're going when we get in there. We just beeline for the table. What do you think, Sara?"

"I think it sounds good. I'm . . . I'm up for it." Sara turned to Sonia. "What do you think? Or do you want to wait for us in the car?"

"Exactly what do you mean by accosting your husbands?" Sonia squeaked. "No, I do not want to sit in the car and wait unless you think I should have the car running for a quick getaway."

Hannah was fuming. "Honey, we will be leaving under our own power, and we won't need a getaway car. Accosting those gentlemen who are our husbands means we will react to the moment, and if certain measures are called for, then we'll . . . we'll do whatever we feel is necessary. Are you okay with that?"

"You bet!"

"Attagirl," Sara said, slapping her sister-in-law on the back. "Okay, let's go!"

They were almost to the door of the Barb Wire and under one of the parking lot lights when Sara looked at Hannah, who in turn was looking at her. Both were wearing bulky ski jackets and wool slacks. Hannah had on one of her homemade knitted caps, whose tassel hung askew. A strand of loose yarn hung down over her left ear. "So we don't look like fashion plates. So what! Ask me if I care."

"It looks pretty crowded," Sonia said uneasily as she looked around the crowded parking lot."

"Good!" Sara and Hannah said in unison.

The Barb Wire was a casual restaurant, with red-checkered tablecloths, peanut shells on the floor, and strings of red chili lights running across and underneath the beams. A barrel of peanuts stood by the hostess table where Angie Loyd was checking off reservations. She looked up as the threesome approached, her face filled with alarm. She knew instantly what was going to go down. Hannah placed her index finger over her lips. Angie nodded before a wide grin split her features. "Give me your things," she whispered. A second later she was holding two jackets and a coat. "Go!" she whispered again.

And go they did.

The table for four was a happy one. Glasses were being raised in a toast. All four diners wore smiles until Joel saw a flurry of movement out of the corner of his eye. He kicked Zack under the table. "I think we have company! This would be a really good time to cut and run, but the exit is blocked. I'm going to kill you, Zack."

Zack turned just in time to see his wife wave airily, an evil smile on her face. His heart started to flutter when he saw the other diners stop eating so they could pay attention to what was going on. "Well, hi!" he said nervously.

"Hi yourself, *Dr.* Kelly," Hannah said, the evil smile still on her face.

Sara moved closer to her husband's chair. "Having a nice time, sweetie? Champagne! Cristal! Oh my goodness. Hannah, they're drinking Cristal at two hundred bucks a pop." Her smile was more evil than her sister's.

"What . . . why don't you girls . . . ah . . .

join us? Listen, Hannah, I can see your brain whirling and twirling. This is not . . . it's not what you think. Is it, Joel?"

"Hell no. This is . . ."

"Spare me, you lowlife weasel," Sara said, backing up a step and shoving Joel so hard he fell.

"I don't want to hear anything out of your mouth either, you . . . you . . . *cur,*" Hannah said.

"I think this might be a good time for us to leave," the blonde said to the redhead.

"Not so fast!" Sonia said, moving to a spot between the two women. She raised her hands and made a fist with each of them. "I might be little, but I'm powerful! I know kung fu!" She did a fast little jiggle, then kicked her right foot out into nowhere. The two women cringed back in their chairs.

"I can explain this . . . Now just a damn minute, Hannah," Zack protested. Hannah's balled-up fist shot forward to land in the middle of her husband's nose. Her evil grin stretched across her face at the sound of crunching cartilage. In a single beat of her heart, her other fist shot out to land directly over Zack's left eye. Not satisfied with the damage she'd done, she hooked her foot under the rung of the chair Zack was sitting on and pushed. He flew forward to land next to Joel, who struggled to get to his feet but couldn't make it. He had two rapidly swelling eyes, and blood dribbled down his chin.

The restaurant was in an uproar as the women cheered and clapped, and the men rushed to the aid of the fallen.

A voice boomed so loud everyone came to a dead stop. *"BACK OFF!"* Sonia, all ninety-seven pounds of her, jiggled and pranced, her legs going in all directions. "Are you finished?" she asked sweetly.

"I am," Hannah said, dusting her hands together. "How about you, Sara?"

"Me too."

At the exit, Sonia turned and said, "There will be no charge for the entertainment this evening, ladies and gentlemen."

"You're a regular spitfire, Sonia," Hannah said as she grabbed her jacket from Angie.

"You're my kind of girl, honey," Sara said, slipping into her jacket. "Does Sam know this side of you?"

"No, but he's going to experience it very shortly."

Hannah burst into tears. "I broke his nose. I heard it crunch."

"So?" Sara said coldly.

"It felt good. I hate myself."

"Shut up, Hannah. We said we were going

to dinner, so let's go. Biffy's Breakfast Bar is open twenty-four/seven. Let's go there. I'll meet you. Oh, look, here come *the girls!* Is that an ambulance I hear? If so, the sheriff will be right behind him. Move, Hannah! Park in the back of Biffy's, where Biff and his wife park."

Both cars were barreling down the side road just as the ambulance and the sheriff's car careened into the parking lot of the Barb Wire.

Fifteen minutes later the three women were settled at a round, scarred table in Biffy's Breakfast Bar, a name that didn't go with the establishment. It was a burger joint with a liquor license, but it did serve egg sandwiches and the best coffee in town in the morning. Just about everyone in town stopped at Biffy's on the way to work in the morning for their first caffeine fix. Biff himself scrutinized the three women with a jaundiced eye. As old and as wise as Cisco, he knew trouble when he saw it.

"Had yourself some excitement over there at the Barb Wire, eh?"

"How . . . how do you know about that so soon?" Sonia gasped.

Biff snorted. "Police scanner. Keep it on day and night. You want some brandy in that coffee?"

"Yeah, but skip the coffee," Hannah said. "No brandy for Sonia, just coffee."

Biff poured liberally. "What are the three of you going to do if those two fine doctors you're married to press charges? Do you want me to call Cisco for you?" Seeing the women's looks of outrage, he discreetly withdrew just as Sara began to have a coughing fit when the brandy seared her throat.

"Oh, God, how did this happen?" Sara moaned as she settled back to normal.

"It just happened. Men get tired of their wives. I guess we're just too ordinary for them. In a million years I could never look like that redhead. The blonde looked like a Las Vegas showgirl. Showgirls are interesting. Men love redheads and blondes, and that blonde didn't look dumb either," Hannah said morosely.

"You know the worst part of all this, Hannah. Cisco and Dad are going to find out. God, can you just imagine the lecture we're going to get. Whose side do you think Sam will be on?"

"What a strange thing to be asking me, Sara. Our side, of course."

"Wrong. Sam had the guts to cut our bond. Sam is his own person these days.

That's a good thing, Hannah. We're on our own."

"No, you aren't. I'm on your side," Sonia said staunchly. "You can always count on me."

"Over Sam?" Sara asked.

"No, not over Sam. That's where we all went wrong. We let each other's lives interfere with our own. What are you two going to do?" Sonia asked.

"I guess I'll take a room at the Inn. I'm sure not going home. How about you, Hannah?"

"My room has two beds. You can stay with me and Sonia. There's no way I'm going to Cisco's or Dad's. And, what about tomorrow? Do we show up, or do we hide out?"

Sara stared at her sister. "Hannah, we aren't the ones who had the affairs. Our husbands had the affairs. We just . . . what we did was . . ."

"Beat the hell out of them in public," Hannah said. "I say we go to the dinner tomorrow and avoid them. No one will say anything with Cisco there. After dinner tomorrow, let's go to New Jersey. Mom needs to know what jerks she left behind. Sonia, don't tell anyone, okay?"

"Okay," Sonia said agreeably.

"I guess we can eat now. Hey, Biff, three

burgers with the works, three loaded baked potatoes, and blue cheese on our salads, and bring us some more coffee!" Sara shouted.

The gymnasium was huge, with a full set of offices, locker rooms, and a large, fully equipped kitchen for events such as this Thanksgiving dinner. During the year the Altar Society, the choir, and the Men's Club held fund-raising events there, for which the women cooked the dinners, and the men served the food. It was the democratic way, Father Stanley said.

The gymnasium, built by the townsfolk, served other purposes, too. It was where Larkspur High held its indoor sports events, held prayer meetings, wedding receptions, and people came when disaster struck. The Christmas and Easter pageants always played to a full house.

Today the gymnasium was decorated for Thanksgiving. The choir members had brought in cornstalks and pumpkins. The Glee Club had festooned the last of the autumn leaves from the rafters and over the doors. Bales of hay with scarecrows in patched outfits graced the four walls. The long tables, with orange-and-gold crepe paper for tablecloths, held rich autumn-colored candles that winked and sparkled.

Crinkly, accordion turkeys sat in the middle of all the tables, with small clusters of pumpkins surrounding their bases. The children would take them home after Thanksgiving dinner. The dishes were orange-and-brown plastic, as was the silverware, all donated by Marion Davis from her gift shop. The Sunday church bulletin would list all the names of those donating goods. All the volunteers' names would be mentioned. The truth was, every person in town's name would be in the bulletin. Father Drupieski was big on democracy and didn't like, as he put it, sourpusses in his congregation.

Thanksgiving dinner was his show, and he reveled in it. Plus, there was nothing he liked more than a big turkey dinner with all the trimmings. The ladies of the Guild were more than kind to him, packaging up dinners that always lasted him into the Lenten season, at which time he switched gears, arranged the Easter dinner, and had ham and sweet potatoes with little marshmallows until the summer harvest. It was a win-win situation that worked just fine for him.

He was walking around the gym, stopping to talk to his parishioners and the few Methodists and Lutherans, along with their respective ministers. He was gracious, as always, in accepting the kind compliments for the warm, cozy turnout and the prospect of an equally wonderful, delicious dinner. As he made his way around the entire gym, his gaze was alert for a sign of the Cisco Trips and Loretta. So far, none of the family had appeared, not even Jonathan. He looked down at his watch. It was two-thirty. Dinner was at three o'clock, but rarely got on the table until four. There was still time for all of them to show up even though Loretta was convinced the Trips would be a no-show, as she put it.

Father Stanley flinched when he heard Clyde Willis strumming on his banjo. For the life of him, he had no idea what the man was playing and seriously doubted if Clyde knew. In his late eighties, Clyde had serenaded the town for over sixty years. So far no one had the nerve to give him the boot. Plus, Clyde was deaf. "I'm taking requests!" Clyde bellowed.

"I'll get back to you on that, Clyde," Father Drupieski said, moving farther away. The old banjo needed tuning. He added that to his mental list of things to take care of in the coming weeks.

Father Stanley moved closer to the kitchen to savor the rich aromas wafting into the gym. He took a minute to look around at his flock. How he loved them, each and every one. He'd christened just about every child there today. Married them, officiated at burials, laughed with them, cried with them, comforted them, always wondering if the words were right. They'd all weathered so much over the years, and yet, there they were, as whole as they could be. Soon it would be time for him to retire. The thought bothered him.

The little church in the valley was now a big church in the valley. He had new parishioners. When it was time to step down, a new priest would come on duty, and another phase of life in the valley would begin. New beginnings. A new beginning was what Loretta Cisco dreaded, what she couldn't come to terms with. "Oh, ye of little faith," he murmured to himself. It would all work out. It always did.

He saw them then, the Trips. They weren't together. Their father, Jonathan, stood near the open doorway with Alice. They looked happy. He hoped Jonathan would get off his duff and ask Alice to marry him. The best thing that could happen to him. And to Alice.

Father Drupieski continued to watch. He convinced himself the Trips were avoiding one another. Where were their spouses? Ah, yes, over at the cider bowl. He frowned at the dark glasses on the two doctors and the patch over Zack's nose. Everybody was avoiding everybody else. Well, that had to stop. He was about to march his way toward the Trips when he felt a hand on his arm.

"Let it go, Drupi. After dinner is time enough. Let's just get through dinner. Then, when the cleanup starts, I'd like you to take my grandchildren in hand. Will you do that for me, Drupi?"

"Of course. Look, Loretta!" Father Stanley said as he pointed a finger across the room. Under the bandstand, Sam and Bill Rutherford were locked in a bear hug that looked fierce. *I wonder what they're saying,* he mused to himself.

Loretta Cisco's shoulders slumped. Hot tears pricked her wrinkled eyelids as she watched the two handsome men across the room pummel each other. The biggest mistake of her life was being rectified in front of her very eyes. Her hand dug into Father Drupieski's arm. "I made so many mistakes, Drupi. So many. Whatever is going on with my beloved Trips is all my fault. I taught them to . . . what I did . . . I let them believe the only people they could trust were each other. Was I blind? Stupid? How could I have done that, Drupi?"

"Sshhh. I think you need to take a step backward now, Loretta, and let those children work it out. You might want to give some thought to the man standing over there by the doorway. I can't swear to this, never having had children, but I think Jonathan could use a few words of praise from his mother. If not now, Loretta, soon."

Cisco dabbed at her eyes before she squared her shoulders. "As usual, Drupi, you're right. It's long overdue." She walked away, stopped, and returned to Father Stanley's side. "It isn't too late, is it, Drupi?"

"Loretta, it's never too late. Not if your heart is in the right place. How many discussions have you and I had on love and faith, trust and forgiveness?"

"Too many for me to remember, old friend."

Across the room, Sam and his new buddy moved away from the crowd. Sam beamed from ear to ear. Bill Rutherford, a silly look on his face, his round glasses steamed up, hung on to Sam's arm as though he was afraid Sam would vanish into thin air.

"I got the first whipping of my life the day I tried to go to your house after my mom's funeral. I was going to ask your mom and dad if I could live with your family."

Bill's eyes sparkled behind his glasses. "No

kidding! Well, I can top that. I got my ass fanned six different times because I high-tailed it to the valley after your mom passed away. Each time I got to the top of the rise, where Ezra's house is, and my dad caught me and dragged me home. He said if your family wanted me there, they would have invited me. Hell, I didn't understand what that meant at the time, so I just kept trying to get to you. One time you three were playing monkey in the middle, and I hollered down to you, but you didn't hear me. I gave up after that. I missed you, Sam. You were my best friend. Oh, I have lots of friends and acquaintances, but no best friend. Except my wife, Julie, of course, but that's different. How about you?"

The expression on Sam's face was that of someone who had found the Holy Grail, a priceless jewel, and Christmas morning all rolled into one. For a few moments he forgot about Sonia and how miserable he'd been. "Nope. Wanna be best buds again?"

"Damn straight I do. We're moving back to the valley next summer. When you have kids, our kids can grow up and play together. You and I will go to ball games with the kids and do all the stuff you and I used to do. Your wife and my wife can hook up and keep our kids on the straight and narrow. Looks like a win-win to me. Maybe that old saying that you can't go home again isn't true. Now, let's go somewhere where we can *really* talk, and you can tell me what it is that's eating you alive."

The relief he felt at his friend's words almost caused Sam to black out. "Won't your wife miss you?"

"Nope. She's in charge of the honey butter for the biscuits. All those women chased me out of the kitchen. Let's go, buddy, we've got some serious talking to do."

It was seven-thirty when the men of the parish bundled up the last of the trash to be taken out to the Dumpster. The tables and chairs had been folded and stored in the storage room until the next big Larkspur event. Only a few stragglers remained, along with Father Stanley's mountain of packaged food. It was Jonathan, Alice at his side, who volunteered to take the packaged dinners to the rectory to store in the freezer.

The Trips were standing with Cisco and Ezra, saying their good-byes. Sonia, Joel, and Zack waited at the door. "Scoot," Cisco said. "Your spouses are waiting for you."

His hungry eyes on his wife, Sam said, "In a minute. Father Stanley said he wanted to talk to us over at the rectory. What did you think of Billy Rutherford, Cisco?"

Cisco stared up at her tall grandson, knowing this was probably the most important question he would ever ask her. Her heart fluttered in her chest. "He looks like a fine young man. Father Stanley said he was moving back to the valley next summer. I'm happy for him and for you, too, Sam. It would be nice if you invited him for Christmas Eve. I'd love for him to come to my wedding Christmas Day. What do you think?" How anxious she sounded. She wondered if Sam was picking up on it.

Sam hugged his grandmother. "I was hoping you'd say that. We'll talk soon, Cisco."

Cisco stared deep into her grandson's eyes. All she saw was love. She almost swooned in relief. "Yes, Sam. You know where to find me."

The Trips moved off. Ezra's comforting hand on her arm calmed Cisco. "See, it wasn't as bad as you thought. Whatever is going on with your grandchildren is being handled by them. They seemed so different today, did you notice? I don't mean that hide-and-seek game they seemed to be playing. Suddenly, at least to me, they looked older, more mature, more . . . I guess the words I'm looking for are . . . *in control.* I think things are going to turn out all right, my dear. I do wonder, though, why those two doctors are wearing sunglasses, and Zack is sporting that bandage over his nose."

Cisco shrugged. Young people today were so strange. "I hope everything does turn out all right. We need to go home, Ezra; the dogs are waiting for us, and we have to feed them. I think it was nice of Emily to bake a chicken for the dogs since dogs aren't supposed to eat turkey. I used to know why that was, but for the life of me, it escapes me at the moment. Emily packaged everything up for them. All we have to do is spoon it out. Freddie does love Thanksgiving dinner with all the trimmings. I know Hugo does, too."

At the door, Cisco kissed everyone and held on to her son longer than she normally did. Tears burned her eyes when she stepped out into the star-filled night. She turned to see the bright lights spilling from the windows in the gymnasium. Soon the building would be dark, and the day would come to an end.

"Do you need a *boost*, Loretta?" Ezra joked. "I can't remember the last time I saw you eat so much. You might be a tad bottom heavy. Two helpings of stuffing!"

"Three!" Cisco said smartly. "And no, I don't need a *boost*, and if you ask me that again, I'll swat you, Ezra."

Ezra smiled in the darkness. "Feels like snow," he muttered as he climbed behind the wheel of the car.

"So it does. Lionel dropped off two cords of wood yesterday. The freezer is full. I have a hundred catalogs to shop from if I want to. It can snow from now till Christmas, and I won't care."

"Uh-huh," was all Ezra said.

Father Stanley waited at the side door while the Trips walked toward him. He squinted behind his wire-rimmed glasses as he watched. How formal they all looked. How reserved. How *damn angry.* They all turned to look at him. He could *feel* their anger and hostility, and it wasn't his imagination either. Maybe anger wasn't the right word. Maybe it was unhappiness. Not satisfied with either assessment, he finally decided what he was seeing was pure, unadulterated *misery.* He waved, then pointed at his watch, which meant, let's get a move on.

The three of them were wary, he'd give them that much. Maybe suspicious. "Let's take this little talk over to the bleachers," he said to them. "I know you all want to go home as badly as I do, but we need to talk before you do that. At least it's warm in here. Now," he said, holding up his hand, "I

212

want to know what's going on with the three of you, and I want to know right now. Pretend this is catechism class, and you've already answered two questions wrong. Bear in mind that I'm not long on patience. I'm waiting."

"With all due respect, Father Stanley, this isn't a confessional, and what right do you have to haul us over here and question us like this? Who put you up to it?" Sara demanded. She hated confrontations almost as much as her siblings did.

"With all due respect, Sassy Sara," Father Stanley said, using her childhood nickname, "I christened you and your brother and sister, so that gives me the right. In addition, your mother asked me to look after you before she died. I promised her I would. You all know how I feel about promises. Now *talk,*" he thundered, his voice ringing in the open expanse of the gymnasium. "And don't leave anything out either."

The triplets eyed him, recognizing the magic words. As one, they started to babble, each one trying to outdo the other.

Drupi felt like he was on a roller coaster to hell as the Trips let loose with finger-pointing, screeching, yelling, name-calling, and using words he suspected weren't in any dictionary. But he was rapidly getting the gist of what was going on. He knew what was coming next, too. He saw Hannah pull back her arm, her hand clenched in a tight fist. He was a split second too late getting off the bleachers. Sam took the blow smack in the middle of his nose. He raised his eyes upward, then threw his hands in the air. The Trips were on a roll, something he'd only heard about. *As Loretta said, it's better for them to play it out than to interfere.*

He'd never really seen the Trips in action, but Loretta had told him about the times they'd pummeled each other. Hearing about it and seeing it were two different things. He knew if he wanted to, he could probably stop it. But did he want to? No, he did not.

Drupi hopped off the bleachers and circled the Trips like a warring referee. They ignored him as they punched, kicked, and gouged one another. "That's it, kill each other, and all your problems are solved!" he bellowed. "C'mon, c'mon, they're just girls, Sam. Sara, you have a better left hook than that! Hannah, you fight like a sissy."

"Shut up, Father," Sam bellowed, as his fist drove into Sara's stomach! Drupi suspected he held back on the punch, but he couldn't be sure.

"Yeah," Sara said.

"This isn't your fight, Father," Hannah

gasped, as Sara's punch knocked her on her fanny. She rolled over grasping her stomach, wailing and threatening her sister with all manner of dire things for the wicked punch.

Father Stanley blessed himself. "The hell it isn't my fight. When I go *up there,* how am I going to explain this to your mother? Huh? Just tell me that." He listened to another blast of verbiage such as he'd never heard before.

Sara limped over to the bleachers and tried to sit down. She failed miserably and landed on her rump. She was bloodied and bruised. "I don't want to do this anymore. Not ever, ever, ever. You started it, Sam."

Hannah tried unsuccessfully to get to her knees. She rolled over and closed her eyes. "This was worse than that Christmas out in the field when we were mad at Dad."

"I hate you both!" Sam said, his ears ringing.

Father Drupieski dropped to his haunches. He clucked his tongue as he looked at Sam's rapidly swelling eyes. He knew the young man's nose was broken. It also looked to him like Sam had fared the worst. Sara's lip was split, and Hannah had a bloody earlobe. Everyone's knuckles were raw and bleeding, their clothes covered in blood. Both Hannah and Sara would sport lovely shiners by morning.

Father Stanley rocked back and forth on his haunches. "I can patch you all up. I've had a lot of experience with the football team, so that's no problem. This way you can avoid having everyone in town know what asses the three of you are. You now know everyone's secrets. You now know who broke their promises. You now know you're all human beings with faults and warts. The blame game is over, boy and girls. This is the *last* time you will *ever* resort to these tactics. Do you hear and understand me?" He listened to the garbled response that sounded like yes to him.

"In addition, I am going to arrange for some counseling for all three of you. It's long overdue. Do you agree to that, too?" Again it sounded like a yes. Father Drupieski ran with his new power. "All right then. Get up, and let's head to the rectory, where I will patch you up. You will sleep at the rectory tonight. Don't even think about saying no. Tomorrow, I am going to drive each one of you home, and I'm going to wait while you talk to your respective spouses. Don't think about objecting. If you want to be treated like an adult, then act like one."

Sam groaned as he tried to get up. He

216

couldn't ever remember being so sore, so battered. When he saw Sara's outstretched hand he turned away. "I don't *need* your help."

"I know, Sam." She didn't take her hand away. Her brother looked into her eyes. He reached for her hand, then was on his feet. They both reached down for Hannah's hands.

"Sonia loves you, Sam. She loves you more than Hannah and I love you. That's a wonderful thing. She's probably too good for you."

"Yes, she is," Sam said, limping to the kitchen doorway, where Father Stanley waited for them.

Outside, in the dark night, Joel and Zack looked at one another in awe. "Let's sit in the car and talk about *this*," Zack said. "Father Stanley said to give him an hour after the kitchen lights go out, then we're supposed to go to the rectory. I don't know if that's a good idea or not. I also don't think he should be the one to explain our situations to our wives. That's something we have to do. There is one bright light here, though."

"Yeah, and that would be . . . what?"

"We'll have matching shiners. Hannah is two for two. She broke my nose, and she broke Sam's nose. They are powerful, I have to admit."

"Shut up, Zack. I hate you or did you forget?" Joel grumbled.

CHAPTER ELEVEN

At ten o'clock Father Drupieski closed his oversize first-aid kit with a loud snap. "I expect the three of you will be a little stiff and sore for a few days, but you'll live. I want to say right now that I do not have one iota, do you hear me, one iota of sympathy for any of you. Now I want you to wait right here till I check with my housekeeper to be sure your rooms are ready. Say some prayers while I'm gone. On second thought, say a lot of prayers while I'm gone."

The moment the door closed, Sara had her jacket on, as did Hanny. "C'mon, Sam, Father Stanley is up to something. That honest face of his gave him away. I bet you a dollar he's got Zack and Joel hiding out in the bushes and went to get them. Move, move! Don't you understand English? Keep quiet when we get outside, too." Sara's voice was so authoritative, both Sam and Hannah obeyed instinctively.

A high wind was rocketing through the parish parking lot as the Trips made their way to their respective vehicles by sliding quietly among the shadows.

Sara pointed to the far side of the rectory, where two figures huddled against the front door. "See! It's that old forgive-and-forget thing Father is so good at. We're going to wait them out even if we freeze out here. Now, remember, keep your voices down," Sara ordered.

"I think it's snowing," Hannah said, holding her face up to feel the tiny flakes. "Hmmm, that feels good."

"Sam, Hannah and I are going to New Jersey now."

Sam gingerly worked his jaw several times before he spoke. "Why?"

"Because. Just me and Sara, Sam."

"Why?" Sam asked again.

"Because you already made the cut. Sonia is at the Inn, Sam. You need to go to her and talk. She's waiting for you. The next time you go to see Mom you can take Sonia and your new baby with you. Right now, Hanny and I *need* to go there; you don't. It's that simple. And, Sam, I'm sorry for all the grief I've given you growing up. Hannah and I were overbearing. It was always two against one. There's a lot of stuff we have to make right in our own lives. You, little brother, are way ahead of us, and that's a really good thing. I just want you to know, we'll always be there for you. Always. But not like before when . . . when we controlled your life. Oh, Sam, I am so very sorry," Sara said, throwing her arms around her brother. Hannah blubbered against his chest, too.

Stunned, Sam wrapped his arms around his sisters. He held them close. "I'll be there for you, too. Say hi to Mom for me, okay? You sure Sonia wants to see me?"

"More than anything in the world, Sam. Just let me give you some advice this one last time, okay, Sam? I'll never offer it again unless you ask. Let Sonia talk. She has a lot to say. That's one dynamite wife you have. Don't let her get away. Pride is a terrible thing. That's all I have to say."

"Sara speaks for me, too, Sam. Oh, look, there *they* go! Wait till they leave the lot before you turn the car on. Good luck, Sam."

A lump the size of a golf ball settled in Sam's throat. "When . . . when are you coming back? What do you want me to say if anyone asks where you went?"

"No more secrets, no more promises, no more don't-tells. It's up to you."

Sam shuffled his feet. "Will you call me when you get there, so I know everything is all right?"

"If you want us to, we will. Don't feel you have to say that. I know old habits die hard, but from here on in it's going to be a learning process for all of us."

"I'm sorry about Zack and Joel. I know that doesn't make you feel any better, but I am sorry."

Hannah rubbed at her eyes. "Go get Sonia, Sam, she's waiting for you."

Sam moved off. He felt strange, almost light-headed, as he watched his sisters settle themselves in the car. He felt relief, sadness, love, and joy. He felt so free he could have taken flight if he had had wings instead of arms. He wanted to sing, to dance, to shout at the top of his lungs. He looked around the dark parking lot. He could do all of those things if he wanted to.

On the second floor of the rectory, Father Drupieski watched from his bedroom window. When he saw the young man down below start to dance and sing to some unheard music, his closed fist shot into the air. "Good for you, Sam!"

The priest crawled into bed, then got back out. He must be in a dither to forget his nightly prayers. How old his bones were, how creaky, how painful.

His prayers finished, he got back into bed. He would sleep now. He knew Sam was going to be all right. Hannah and Sara were on their way to the only place that could give them the comfort and solace they needed at the moment. The boys, that was how he thought of Zack and Joel, would be all right, too. Embarrassed but all right. It seemed to him everyone had learned a hard lesson on this special Thanksgiving Day. As he blessed his pillow and himself one more time, he allowed himself a small wish. He wished for a dog. Someone to keep him company. Someone to listen to his ramblings. Someone to keep his feet warm in bed. He was trying to remember how many times he'd made the same wish, but he fell asleep. It never occurred to him that all he had to do was to voice his wish aloud, and he would be surrounded by a houseful of dogs. But Father Stanley Drupieski never, ever asked anything for himself, only for others.

Sonia walked over to the door the moment she heard the light knock. She opened it and had to fight with herself not to rush into her husband's arms. "Hello, Sam." She eyed his battered face but made no other comment.

"Can I come in, Sonia?"

"Why? It's late, Sam. I was just getting ready for bed."

"Why? Because I need to talk to you, that's why. I have things I need to say. I imagine you have things you want to say to me. I want to tell you how much I love you. I want to tell you how much I missed you. I want to tell you I'm happy about the baby. Stuff like that."

"Very well. Come in. I'll listen to what you have to say. I will not make any promises, Sam. Do you still want to come in?"

"Yes. Yes, I do."

"All right." Sonia held the door open and motioned Sam to one of the dark green chairs sitting next to the table. She sat down in the chair opposite her husband and folded her arms.

"I'm really sorry, Sonia. I thought . . . damn, I thought all kinds of things. Having children so soon wasn't in my life plan. We both agreed to wait a while. I took your getting pregnant as a betrayal on your part. That was so wrong of me. But it was wrong of you to lie to me and run off, too. If it takes me the rest of my life, I'll make it up to you. I want this baby, Sonia. I want to be a father. In some crazy way I was trying to avoid being a father because of my own father. I have stuff in my head that's been locked away from the time my mother died. I'm taking it out, a little at a time, and looking at it. Sara, Hannah, and I all agreed with Father Stanley that we need some counseling. I've got a bead on it, but I'm going anyway. It was never you, Sonia. It was me."

"Then I can get a job and earn a paycheck?"

Sam blinked. "If that's what you want, it's fine with me. By March of next year, Sara will have the company's day-care center up and running. She's about to start interviewing for a director. You more than qualify, Sonia, but, of course, the decision is up to you."

"Then why did you give me so many arguments before I left when I said I wanted to work."

Sam swiped at his curls. "I thought you wanted to stay home."

"No, Sam. *You* wanted me to stay home. Because your mother stayed home and didn't work. My parents sacrificed a lot to send me here to college. I want to work so I can repay them some of the money. I tried telling you that, but you ignored me."

Sam nodded. "I did do that, didn't I? I'm sorry, Sonia. You're right, I was trying to recapture a time in my life when I was totally happy. Mom was always home when we came in from school. She always baked and ironed and did all those things that I wanted you to do. I guess I was pretty stupid. I suppose there's a lot of other stuff I didn't *hear,* too."

"Yes, Sam, a lot of stuff as you say. The big thing was . . . is, you didn't trust me, and now you want me to trust you. You're saying words, Sam. How do I know you mean them? A baby is going to change our lives. I have no intention of being a stay-at-home mom. I can do it on my own. I can return home. I have other options."

"I know you do, Sonia. Can't you see your way clear to giving me a chance? I don't want to lose you because of my stupidity."

Sonia allowed a small smile to tug at the corners of her mouth. "Are you telling me you are smart now?"

Sam grinned. "A little smarter. Guess what, Sonia, I met up with Billy Rutherford. I met his wife, and she's about due to have a baby. You'd like her. They're moving back here to the valley. They could become good friends and be part of our new life. Will you at least think about all this?"

"I'll think about it, Sam. No promises, though."

"Okay. When . . . when do you think you'll . . . you know, make up your mind?"

"Close your eyes, Sam." Sam closed his eyes.

"Open your eyes, Sam." Sam opened his eyes.

"I swear, every time I look at you, you get prettier. I heard what a tiger you were last night at the Barb Wire. I didn't know you were such a wild woman. That's a compliment," he added hastily.

Sonia nodded, accepting the compliment. "I've decided. I'll give you another chance."

Sam picked up his tiny wife and swung her off the floor before he planted a kiss on her lips that made Sonia swoon with pleasure. He set her down, looked deeply into her eyes, and said, "This has to wait. I have to go and see Zack and Joel. I owe my sisters that much. You want to come along?"

"Oh, yes. Yes indeedy. I, too, would like to give those two *oafs* a piece of my mind. I thought so much more of them. I would never have believed they would betray their wives like that, but I saw the women with my own eyes. They looked so . . . so guilty."

"*Oafs* is it?" Sam grinned. "Let's get their side of it. Sara said they were trying to explain, but my sisters wouldn't listen."

Sonia sniffed. "I can't even begin to

imagine how they could defend having affairs. For professional men, doctors no less, how could they do such a thing?"

"I don't know, but we're going to find out right now. Dress warm, honey, it's cold outside. Sonia, do you have any idea how much I love you?"

"Yes, Sam, because I love you just as much."

Five minutes later they were on their way to Zack Kelly's house.

With few cars on the road at that late hour, Sam felt confident enough to hold the steering wheel in his left hand while he held his wife's hand with the other. From time to time, he squeezed it. Both of them were smiling in the darkness. "Do you think it will be a boy or a girl?"

Sonia laughed. "I don't know. It doesn't matter as long as the baby is healthy."

"Yeah, yeah, that's how I feel."

"Looks to me like Zack is still up. Guess he can't sleep," Sam said, turning into his brother-in-law's driveway. "That's Joel's car. Misery does love company. Now look, Sonia, if this little visit turns physical, I don't want you to get involved. Understood?"

"Understood, Sam."

Together, they walked up to the front door

and rang the bell. A battered Zack glared at them in the open doorway. "What the hell do you want now, Sam? Did you come here to gloat or to take a shot at me, too?"

"I don't know yet, Zack. There's three sides to everything. Your side, my sister's side, and the truth, which lies somewhere in the middle. I'm here to hear what you and Joel have to say."

"Why bother, Sam? You already made up your mind to believe your sisters," Zack snarled, his face grimacing in pain.

An equally battered Joel popped around the corner. "What?" he bellowed. "Are you here to beat us to a pulp, too?"

"No. Listen, it's cold out here. Can we come in?"

"Well sure, Sam. Joel and I have just been sitting here waiting for you to show up." His sarcasm was not lost on Sam, who ushered Sonia into the warm house ahead of him.

Sam and Sonia sat on one sofa, Joel and Zack on the opposite sofa. A huge fire burned in the fireplace. They all glared at one another.

"Talk," Sam said, menace ringing in his voice.

The two doctors babbled as one as Sam stared at both his brothers-in-law in stupefied amazement.

When they finally wound down, Sam said, "Let me get this straight. This is all about you two buying a boat you are going to pick up in Miami the first week in January. You are both taking a year's leave to sail. However, you neglected to tell your wives because you felt guilty after you did it. How'm I doing so far?" Neither doctor answered him.

"So, the two women you were having dinner with yesterday evening were delivering your certificates for all the courses you've taken over the past few months. The gift boxes were captain's hats, compliments of the dealer you bought the boat from. The women, Marylee and Corinne, were your boating instructors. That's it!"

"Every last bit of it."

"And you two did not have affairs with those women is what you're telling me."

Disgust washed over both doctors' faces. "Sam, take a look at these papers. It says right at the top how many hours are required for each course. When in the hell would we have had time to have affairs? There aren't enough hours in the day for something like that. On top of that, I take my wedding vows seriously," Zack said.

"We were going to tell Sara and Hannah

this weekend, but things got out of hand. We're guilty of being stupid, but that's all we're guilty of. Now, go home and leave us to our misery," Joel said.

"This is pretty impressive," Sam said as he held up the thick sheaf of certificates that said both Joel and Zack were advanced enough to take a boat out onto the water and live to return to port. "What are you going to do now?"

"Hide out until we can go out in public without scaring people," Zack snapped. "After that, I plan to try and explain to Hannah. If she chooses not to listen, I'm leaving with Joel the first week in January. It's my dream, Sam. Something I've wanted all my life, and I'm not giving it up."

Sam propped his elbows on his knees. "And you shouldn't have to give it up. Want some advice?"

"No!" both doctors shouted in unison.

"I'm going to give it to you anyway. Now listen up." As he talked, he was drawing a road map. "At best they have an hour to an hour and a half start. Sara obeys the speed limit, and they like to stop every fifty miles or so for bathroom breaks. I bet you anything you could get there before they do if you leave right now."

Joel had his jacket on before Sam stopped

speaking. Zack zipped up his own jacket, throwing one of Hanny's mufflers around his neck.

"Lock up, Sam," Zack shouted over his shoulder.

"This is so bizarre," Sonia said. "Another example of what happens when married couples don't communicate." It was said coolly and pointedly.

Sam nodded. "Point taken."

"Let's go home, Sam."

"Sonia, those are the sweetest-sounding words I've ever heard in my life."

Joel looked down at the oversize watch on his wrist. "It's a quarter to four, Zack, and I'm so cold I think my blood froze in my veins an hour ago. Either we missed them, or they aren't going to come here till morning. The flip side of that is old Sam might have snookered us. I saw a twenty-four-hour diner back there on Route 27. Let's get some coffee and try to warm up."

"I'm not going anywhere until my wife gets here. You can go if you want to. I'm positive Sam didn't snooker us. Bear in mind we probably broke about twenty speed laws getting here. Like Sam said, Sara obeys the speed limit. Oh, oh, I see headlights. Duck behind that big stone over there, Joel."

Joel obeyed his friend. "How do you know it's *them?*"

"Who else but our wives would come here in the middle of the night. On the other hand, it might be the cops. Shut up and let's see what's going on here."

"They're going to see our car," Joel hissed.

"No they aren't. I can't even see it from here. In case you haven't noticed, the lot is pitch-black. Do you know why it's pitch-black, Joel? It's pitch-black because there are no lights, and the reason there are no lights is because normal, sane people don't go to cemeteries in the middle of the night except on Halloween, and it isn't Halloween. It's *them!*"

Zack kept his eyes glued to the huge stone in front of him. He wondered who Dennis and Madeline Baker were. Joel poked him in the ribs, and hissed, "Listen."

Both doctors hunched together. From time to time they wiped at the corners of their black-and-blue eyes, both feeling lower than a snake's belly. When the anguished outpouring of sadness on the other side of the narrow row of stones stopped, Zack sucked in his breath and let loose with a litany of sorrow directed at Dennis and Madeline Baker. He confessed everything from the moment he and Joel looked at the catalog with the boat they eventually bought. He was breathless when he wound down, his fingers tracing the names of Dennis and Madeline, and apologizing to the unknown persons resting beneath the ground.

When he looked up, his wife was staring down at him, her expression unfathomable in the darkness. "You bought a ship!"

"Boat. It's a boat, Hanny. The *QE2* is a ship."

"I get seasick," Hanny said quietly.

"They . . . they have a patch for that. I have a whole box. So does Joel. A hundred to a box," Zack said, desperation ringing in his voice. "It's always been a dream of mine. The kind of dream that if you don't snatch it when it appears, you never get another chance at. I snatched it, Hanny."

Hannah dropped to her knees. "Why didn't you trust me enough to tell me? All I ever wanted was what you wanted, for you to be happy. If you're happy, I'm happy."

"Probably for the same reason you didn't trust me. How could you have been so quick to think I would have an affair?"

"I guess we're both pretty stupid. It's hard for me . . . to . . . trust other people. All our lives, Sam, Sara, and I only trusted each other. Sam . . . Sam figured it all out way ahead of us. You aren't off the hook, though. This is going to take some getting used to. You're asking me to give up my life for a whole year. That means I'll have to leave Cisco in the lurch. Sara will, too. Those two women we saw with you at the restaurant are beautiful."

"Yes, they are. That's one of the reasons they're so good at what they do. They sell boats, then they teach the classes. Both of them are happily married, Hanny, and both of them have two kids each. Beauty is in the eye of the beholder as you know. I wouldn't trade you for a dozen boats and fifty women that look like Marylee and Corinne. I mean that, Hanny. Listen, you're going to have to help me up. I'm so cold I can't move."

"Wuss," Hanny said, holding out her hand. "I'm glad you came, Zack."

"Yeah, me too. Can we go now?" Hannah started to walk away. Zack turned back to the gravestone where he'd been hiding. His hand reached out to touch the carved letters. His hand almost went to the name Dennis, but at the last second he moved his fingers closer to the name Madeline. He didn't know how he knew, but he knew that Dennis was a tyrant and that Madeline was a sweet soul. His finger gently traced the long name. "Thanks for listening, Madeline.

I'll be back sometime, and we'll talk again. I have a feeling you're hearing me. I gotta go now, Madeline, my wife is waiting for me."

Sara looked up at her tall husband and smiled. "Well, Captain Marvel, I think we both learned a lesson. I'm sorry I didn't trust you, honey. It's all part of being a set of triplets if you can understand that. All our lives we thought for one another. There were no outsiders in our lives to show us differently. The three of us have seen the error of our ways, and it will never happen again. It's . . . it's so hard to let go of something that's worked for you all your life. Sam learned it first, Hanny second, and me last. I like it this way, I really do. Forgive me?"

"Oh, yeah," Joel said, kissing her soundly. "Hmmm, you taste like strawberries."

"Keep nibbling, honey, keep nibbling." Sara laughed.

CHAPTER TWELVE

Half-awake, half-asleep, Sara stretched out under the warm covers before she rolled over on her side to peer at the digital alarm clock with its red numerals. Seven o'clock. She heard the shower running and smiled. Usually she was the first one up to put the coffee on. She could smell it now. Leaning back into her warm nest beneath the covers, she continued to smile. This past month rivaled her honeymoon. After the debacle of the boat, both Joel and she had worked overtime to please one another. They'd made earth-shattering promises to each other that both intended to keep.

Now, here it was, Christmas Eve. Where did the month go?

She really should get up. There was so much to do. Joel would help her, though. His last day at the hospital had been four days ago. He was now a free agent, a free spirit, a nomad, and full of wanderlust, as he put it. Ten more days, and they would head south for Miami. She couldn't wait, and yet she felt disloyal for her wild anticipation. A whole year to do absolutely nothing but spend time with her husband.

She had to admit that at first she had felt a reasonable amount of fear and trepidation, just as Hannah did. But, holding her marriage together was the most important thing in the world to her. If she had one wish this Christmas season, it would be that Cisco would be a little more enthusiastic and embrace the idea. Not so her father, who shouted his approval and bellowed at the top of his lungs that with no children in their lives they should all follow their dream.

Joel emerged from the bathroom, a large yellow towel wrapped around his middle. How good he looked. How *delicious*. She beckoned him with the crook of her finger.

"Oh, no. We have a ton of stuff to do today, Sara. Besides, I'm making breakfast since it's my turn." Joel threw open the drapes. Sara gasped as she hopped out of bed.

"How much is out there? It must have started to snow during the night, after we went to bed."

"A couple of inches. If we hurry, we can do everything we have to do before the roads get bad. Move your tush, Sara."

" 'Move your tush, Sara,' is that what you said, honey?"

In the blink of an eye, Sara had the yellow towel in her hands as she twirled away, then jumped in the middle of the bed. "Ooohhh," she gurgled. "Wanna try that *WOW* thing?" Joel groaned before he took a Tarzan leap, beating his chest at the same time.

"Oooh, oooh," her husband said as he collapsed on top of her.

A long time later, they both stirred at the same time. "This is so wonderful, isn't it, Joel?"

"Yes. The last six months were so grueling, I didn't know which end was up. There are no words to tell you how glad I am that this whole sorry mess came to a head. I am so looking forward to this coming year. Ben promised to dress up for the kids just the way I did. He's good with them, too. He's also going to have all the help he needs with favors other doctors owe him and me. I know I'm leaving my practice in good hands, just the way Zack is leaving his practice to Jonesy. When we get back, I'm going to start interviewing for another associate, or at least a physician's assistant. Working twenty-four/seven just doesn't cut it when you're married.

239

"Another thing, Sara, I don't want you to feel you have to go to nursing school just so you can work with me. I made a promise to you that I would cut back my hours as much as I can."

"Nope. I'm going back to school. I want to be part of your life. I think I'll make a good nurse. My mom was a nurse, did you know that? She had to give up nursing when we came along, though."

"We should get up," Joel said.

"Yes, we should," Sara said.

Joel stared out the window. "Let it snow, let it snow, let it snow," he murmured as he nuzzled his wife's ear.

"None of that, Dr. Wineberg. We really have to get moving, and you're cooking breakfast. I will make you an offer you can't refuse, though. Let's take a shower together. I'll wash your back if you wash mine."

"That's the second best offer I've had today," Joel said, streaking for the shower.

Two streets away, Hannah and Zack Kelly stood in their living room trying to decide which car to take to run their last-minute Christmas errands. Zack's foot prodded one of the piles of gaily wrapped presents.

"Christmas is going to be different this year," Hannah said, sadness ringing in her

240

voice. "I know we're all going to be together, but it's going to be different. We won't be making the taffy we make every year because the copper pot and the paddle blew away in the tornado. Cisco doesn't have the heart for much of anything this season. She's trying, but I can tell it's an effort. And she's getting married tomorrow. I think we're all overwhelmed this year."

Zack wrapped his arm around his wife's shoulder. "Christmas will be whatever we all make it. It's going to be a white one, that's for sure. It's amazing how it always snows in the valley for Christmas."

"We've always had a white Christmas for as long as I can remember. I'm not sure if Cisco is really all right with the four of us heading south after New Year's. She said she is, but I think she feels she has to say that. Dad is more than okay with it."

"Stop worrying, Hanny. Everything is going to work out just fine. Be thankful all your family will be together. Hell, I don't even know where my family is. They all go somewhere for the holidays. For some reason being home for the holidays was never important to them. It was to me, though. Unfortunately for me, no one cared enough to ask my opinion, so I had to fend for myself."

"That's never going to happen again. My family is your family. I think we should get started. Father Stanley gave me the Christmas list two weeks ago. Take a count, Zack. We have to make sure we get everything right. The families know we're coming, so they'll be ready for the food baskets. The toys, the bikes, and the scooters are to go in garages. Father marked those with a red X. Sara's got the computer that goes to the Davenports in her car. Sam has six bikes on top of his truck. I've got all the doll babies and gear in my car, so I guess I'll just follow you. We really are going to need two cars."

"Don't forget we have to pick up Father Stanley's present before three o'clock."

Hannah grinned from ear to ear. "It's so nice playing Santa, isn't it?"

"Yes, it is. Okay, Mrs. Claus, let's get this show on the road."

Giggling like a little girl, Hannah gathered up two of the food baskets and carried them out to her car.

An hour later, a car horn sounded at the end of the Kellys' driveway. Four vehicles were lined up waiting for Zack and Hannah.

The family.

Cisco glared at the new stove, the oven in particular. "I don't know, Ezra, you can only roast two things in this newfangled oven. We could have used the oven in your house. Now, why didn't I think about that earlier?"

"Because your mind is a million miles away, that's why, Loretta. We're just having family and Father Stanley, so that prime rib will be more than enough. You baked your pies and rolls this morning, so what else do you need to roast or bake?"

"Nothing, I suppose. The table's set. I guess there's nothing for us to do but sit down and stare at our Christmas tree. It's not very big, Ezra."

"It's eight feet, Loretta," Ezra said patiently. "You're just upset because no one came to help us decorate it. It's pretty, even though all the ornaments and lights are new. The family will love it. The lights Hugo found are glowing beautifully around the lamppost at the end of the driveway. We need to be thankful, Loretta, that the whole family will be here. I don't want to hear another word about not being able to make the taffy this year."

"All right, Ezra. The house smells nice,

doesn't it? The balsam almost covers the new-wood-and-paint smell. I miss Hannah and Sarah already, and they haven't even gone yet. How can that be, Ezra?"

Ezra pulled his pipe out of the pocket of his red flannel shirt. He tapped down the tobacco and fired up his pipe.

"That's such a bad habit," Cisco sniffed.

"I'm thinking you could do with one or two bad habits yourself," Ezra sniffed in return. "Maybe you should think about doing something really dangerous, like painting your toenails red or something equally decadent."

Cisco burst out laughing as she threw a dish towel at the man she was marrying on Christmas Day. She thanked God that Ezra had come into her life. Without him, she knew she would have collapsed after the tornado. He kept her grounded, as Sam put it.

"Why don't you and I have a nice glass of brandy, Ezra? We can use that brand-new decanter and our brand-new brandy snifters. I'd like to make a toast to you for putting up with me these past weeks. I know it wasn't easy. Sshhh," she said, when Ezra was about to protest. "It's true. I felt so sorry for myself, I didn't see how unhappy my Trips were. Oh, I saw things, but chose not to act on them. It was the same with Jonathan. Drupi helped me a lot, you know. He listened till his ears ached. Poor man. I thought he'd be here by now."

"It's not five o'clock yet, Loretta. The Trips are out doing his bidding. I'm sure he's waiting to see that everything goes off as scheduled. Plus, it's snowing out there. I hope we don't have to put dinner on hold again this year to pull someone out of a snowdrift."

Cisco handed Ezra the brandy snifter. She raised her own glass to clink against his. "To the man I want to spend the rest of my days with if he'll have me." A lone tear trickled out of the corner of her eye to match the one on Ezra's cheek. Together, they sat down on the new sofa. Both dogs jumped up to be beside them.

"See, Loretta, our immediate family is right here. For now, it's all we need."

It was true, and Cisco knew it. "Wanting others' happiness is all that's important. Knowing when to let go makes for that happiness. That's what you're saying to me, isn't it, Ezra?"

"I guess so. I'm not as good with words as you are, Loretta."

"They'll do, Ezra, they'll do."

The five vehicles lined up in front of the rectory. It was decided among the six people in those vehicles that Sam would take the crossed-off list of Christmas deliveries to Father Drupieski by way of the back door. Zack, the fastest on his feet, would then deliver their present to the front door and ring the bell, at which point he would high-tail it around the side of the building where his car was parked. Sam would stay just long enough to make sure the present was taken inside out of the cold and snow.

"Okay, gang, let's do it!" Sam bellowed as he beelined through the snow to the back door of the rectory. The minute the priest opened the door, Sam shoved the lists into his hands. "We ran a little late, Father, but we made every delivery. Listen, do you need a ride out to the valley? I can take you if you're ready."

"No, that's okay, Sam. Toby came by before he closed the garage and put chains on my car. I like driving through town looking at all the lights. I won't be late. Go on now, go home to your wife and family. I'll see you in a little while."

"Oh, I hear your front doorbell! You better go see who it is, Father."

"Yes, I guess I had better do that. You're a good boy, Sam."

For no reason, Sam felt tears burn his eyes. "You know what, Father Stanley, you're an okay guy yourself. Boy, it's cold out here. You better not keep whoever it is at your door waiting. See ya later."

Sam slipped and slid his way around to the front in time to see Father Drupieski open the door, look down, pick up the basket, and carry it inside. He whooped his pleasure as he made his way to his truck. *Damn, I feel good.*

Inside the rectory, Father Stanley carried the heavy basket out to the kitchen, where he set it on the table. Some kind parishioner sending him Christmas dinner no doubt. He removed the light covering and stared down at the contents, his jaw dropping in amazement. Two tiny, fuzzy little heads bobbed up immediately.

"Dogs!" Drupi shouted. "Two dogs!" He scooped the warm balls of fur into both his hands and brought them up to his cheeks, his eyes raised heavenward. "How *did* you know?" he asked over and over. "Well this is certainly going to make life interesting," he said, happier than he'd ever been. "Are you boys or girls? Not that it matters. I think, since I don't know the first thing about puppies, I am going to bundle you back up and get some advice from an authority, Loretta Cisco."

On his way out to his old car to warm it up, Father Stanley sang a robust chorus of "Jingle Bells." His stride was peppy even though he was trudging through the snow. His heart was lighter than it had been in months. And all because someone, somewhere, knew and cared enough to grant his unspoken wish. Who? Did it really matter? He decided it didn't as he scurried back to his new roommates.

Loretta Cisco's eyes sparkled as she looked around at her happy, laughing family. Piles of presents nestled under the tree. The huge gold star from Wal-Mart glistened in the glow of the colored lights at the top of the tree. The tree looked festive. There were nine additional ornaments hanging on it, each with meaning from the giver. "In twenty years, we'll be able to fill up a twenty-footer," Sam joked. "Hey, I don't see Father Stanley. Do you think he got lost in the snow? You might have to go out to look for him, Ezra." He winked slyly at Zack, who was grinning from ear to ear.

"I hear him now," Ezra said. "No one else

in town has a car horn that says, *tootaloo!* Stay put, everyone, I'll open the door.

The piles of presents under the tree suddenly seemed pale by comparison to Father Stanley's Christmas present as everyone gathered around to peer into the basket.

"My goodness, Drupi, you must have been really good to get such a present. It's warm in here, and the fire is going. Take them out of the basket and let them play a little," Cisco said, all smiles. "Freddie and Hugo won't hurt them. Do they have names?"

"Names?" Drupi dithered. "No. Not yet. Oh, dear, the fat one just peed on your carpet, Loretta."

Cisco laughed in delight. "So it did. Let's just say your pup christened my carpet. Freddie did that when I first got her. Oh, oh, there goes the other one." She laughed again. "Oh, Drupi, how wonderful for you."

"I wish I knew who it was that gave me these beautiful pups. I'd like to thank them. I've been wishing for years for a dog," Father Stanley continued to dither, as the frisky pups scooted around the floor, Freddie and Hugo hot on their trail. When the fat one peed again, Freddie barked and nudged her toward the door.

"It doesn't matter. It simply doesn't matter," Cisco said happily, as Ezra mopped up the wet spots. "Now, I think we should get ready for dinner. Everything is piping hot and ready to put on the table."

Mass confusion reigned as everyone got in everyone else's way, but finally dinner was on the table. Father Stanley bowed his head, said grace, then smiled at everyone. "Merry Christmas to you all."

Two hours later, in the middle of the cleanup, Cisco drew Sam to the side. "Put your coat on, Sam. I want you to follow me out to the barn." Puzzled, Sam obeyed his grandmother, worry clouding his eyes. He didn't ask questions.

"My goodness, it's cold. I hope we can make it to the church tomorrow for my wedding."

"Not to worry, Cisco, I'll carry you if I have to." Sam grinned. "What is it you want me to see, Cisco?"

"This," Cisco said, walking over to an old plank table. She pointed to a cardboard box. In the dim light, Sam could make out the lettering on top of the box. SAM'S HAPPY CLOTHES.

Sam's hands shook as he removed the cover and stared down at piles of neatly folded clothing. His old clothes. "You saved my happy clothes," he said, awe written all over his face. "I guess I should ask, why?"

"I don't know. Maybe I knew this day was going to come. I don't know, Sam, I just did."

"I don't know what to say. This is better than . . . than . . . my first bike, my first car. Damn, it's better than anything in the world." He hugged his grandmother so hard she begged for mercy.

"I'm just glad the barn didn't get destroyed in the tornado. Your father said it can be shored up and repaired in the spring. My first thought when I realized everything was gone was that the contents of the barn were intact."

"As Father Stanley says, God does work in mysterious ways. This," he said, pointing to the box, "and Father Stanley's pups."

Cisco smiled. Like she didn't know who gave Drupi the pups. "We should go back inside. It's time to open the presents."

Sam peered down at his grandmother. "We're not leaving you, Cisco. We'll always be here, but our lives are a little fuller, the hours more demanding. I'll do a good job running the company. Sonia is so happy that she can operate the day-care center. Betty Thatcher is stepping in for Sara and Teresa Murray is taking over for Hannah. That leaves Dad."

Cisco linked her arm with Sam's. "I got it covered, Sam."

"Merry Christmas, Cisco."

"Merry Christmas, Sam."

Inside, everyone was seated as they waited for Cisco and Sam. No one asked questions. The pups were busy tripping and tumbling through the piles of presents, tugging on the colored ribbons and chewing at the corners of the gifts. Freddie and Hugo looked tired as they did their best to keep track of their new charges.

"I have to go outside for my presents," Jonathan said. "Sam, want to help me?"

"Sure, Dad."

They were back within minutes, Jonathan holding a cradle and Sam carrying a huge wooden paddle. Sonia and Cisco burst into tears at the same moment as everyone in the room ooohed and aaaahed over the detail on the cradle and the paddle.

"Son, it's an exact replica of the first paddle I used to stir the taffy when I started Cisco Candies. How can I ever thank you?"

"I loved doing it, Mom. I scoured this state trying to find a copper pot like the one you had, but I couldn't find one. I'll keep looking. I know what the pot and paddle meant to you."

"Everyone, open mine next," Hannah

shouted. "Mine are the ones with the satin ribbon. C'mon, c'mon, I spent a whole month on them." She held her breath, waiting for the first person to open their present. Sam won.

"It's a scarf," Sam said. "You give me a scarf every year."

"And . . ."

"And . . . and there are no holes in it!" Sam exclaimed. "Oh, my, God, Hanny, you made a perfect scarf! I don't believe it."

Everyone chorused at once, "Mine's perfect, too!"

"Anyone can make a perfect scarf. I like the one where you sewed buttons to cover the holes. It's a great conversation piece. I'll save this perfect one for special occasions."

Sonia held up a baby blanket that was so exquisite she had tears in her eyes. "It's the most beautiful blanket I've ever seen. I'll treasure it, Hannah, as will our first baby."

Hanny glowed with pleasure.

Gift opening took another hour before it was time to head to church for midnight mass. While everyone was getting dressed, Cisco led her son out to the kitchen. "I have something for you, son, but first I want to thank you again for the paddle and to tell you how sorry I am that you didn't get to follow your dream. It's so strange how at my age I am learning new things every day. I also want to thank you for all the hard work you did with the houses. I'm not sure, Jonathan, that I ever truly knew building was such a passion with you. So, now that I know, I'm firing you and giving you this," she said, extending a long white envelope.

Jonathan's hands trembled as he opened the envelope to look at the deed to the fifty-acre parcel of land on the other side of the valley. "Mom, are you sure you want to do this?"

"Jonathan, I am more than sure. Giving you your dream, even if it is at this late date, gives me great pleasure. Merry Christmas, son."

"Merry Christmas, Mom."

The Wedding of the Year got off to a slow start because of the heavy snow. The men of the Cisco family spent three hours pulling vehicles out of snowbanks and rescuing stranded guests. Ezra was so tired, he had to be helped down the aisle, and Jonathan had to hold him while he said his vows. The vows were no sooner over than Ezra perked up and waltzed down the aisle with his new bride, singing at the top of his lungs. Cisco joined in as did all their friends. They were still singing as they put on winter coats and galoshes to trek from the church to the auditorium, where the whole town turned out to toast their wedding.

The Trips and the townsfolk had helped decorate the auditorium the day before the wedding. Huge red bows, garlands of balsam and white satin bows were everywhere because that's what Cisco had requested.

Huge buffet tables were laden with turkey, prime rib, and shrimp. It was all what Cisco and Ezra called down-home food.

The music was provided by half the high school band, the half that pretended they were musicians. They were loud, off-key, and the singer didn't have the words down pat, but no one minded. Drupie was called into service when some of the older members wanted to slow dance. He cranked up his ancient Victrola and pulled out his equally ancient scratchy records. No one minded that either.

"Group picture! Group picture!" Jonathan shouted. A mad scurry followed as Cisco, Ezra, Jonathan, the Trips, and their spouses stood in front of the Christmas tree."

"Oh, Cisco, it was such a great idea for all of us to wear these little red capes with the white bunny fur and these matching Santa hats! Now *this* is a wedding!" Hanny cried happily.

"Wedding outfits can be so boring," Cisco said. "I wanted to dress mine up a little. It is Christmas! Wait! Wait! Freddie! Hugo!"

Both dogs raced across the auditorium, wearing red-and-green neckerchiefs and matching Santa hats, to stand in front of the bride and groom.

"Now, we're all here! Hit it, Drupie!" Cisco shouted as she boldly waved her hand to show off her new wedding ring.

Everyone in attendance begged to have a copy of the picture sent to them. Father Drupie promised to put copies in the back of the church, where they could be picked up after Sunday mass.

Cisco broke tradition then because everyone stood in a circle. She tossed her bridal bouquet of poinsettias high in the air. Alice caught it simply by reaching forward and snagging it from Stella Abernathy, who pouted all evening because she didn't catch it.

Fred, the lead trombone player from the school band, and his Merry Minnows, struck up a chorus of a song no one could identify, but the guests started dancing, and one and all, had a rousing time.

EPILOGUE

It was a perfect June day with a summer blue sky and golden sunshine. A light breeze caressed the boat's passengers as they maneuvered *The Madeline Baker,* also known as Zack and Joel's boat, into its slip.

Hannah, brown as a berry, jumped onto the dock just as her cell phone rang. The others stopped to listen when they heard her say, "Who is this? What? Can you speak more clearly? Sam! Is that you, Sam? It is you. Okay, we've established you're you. What's wrong? Wrong, Sam? What's wrong? You helped! You!

"Oh my gosh! How much? You have to be kidding! You aren't kidding! When?"

"What?" those standing on the dock shouted.

Hannah turned around, her face alight with happiness. "Hold on a minute, Sam. Sam and Sonia are the new parents of twin boys, six pounds each. They were born an hour ago. Sam helped during the delivery. Sonia is fine. Sam's a wreck. He's going to send us the newborn picture digitally as soon as we can hook up our laptop computers."

"We'll be there, Sam. We'll be the ones with bells around our necks. Nice going, little brother!"

"We're aunts," Hannah said hugging Sara. "You guys are uncles! The christening is in three weeks. We have to go back for it. Sam said he's going to call the boys Frick and Frack. Sonia said no he isn't. He will. You wait and see! Oh, this is so wonderful!"

Arm in arm, the foursome walked up the dock to search out a hotel.

"Our family is growing," Sara said happily.

"Oh my gosh. We have to find a store. I need to make another blanket!" Hannah said.

"Whatever you want, honey, whatever you want," Zack said, reaching for her hand. "When are you going to tell them we're next?"

"Any minute now," Hanny gurgled with happiness. "Any minute now."

Sara turned, "Joel and I have something to tell you two."

"Oh, no, you aren't beating us to it. We're

pregnant!" Hannah shouted.

"So are we," Sara said, doubling over with laughter.

The employees of Thorndike Press hope you have enjoyed this Large Print book. All our Thorndike, Wheeler, and Kennebec Large Print titles are designed for easy reading, and all our books are made to last. Other Thorndike Press Large Print books are available at your library, through selected bookstores, or directly from us.

For information about titles, please call:
  (800) 223-1244

or visit our Web site at:
  http://gale.cengage.com/thorndike

To share your comments, please write:
  Publisher
  Thorndike Press
  10 Water St., Suite 310
  Waterville, ME 04901